THE PURSUIT OF REVENGE

Harvey Sagar

Published by Harvey Sagar
ISBN: 978-1-9998573-3-2
Copyright 2020. All rights reserved
www.harveysagar.com

Chapter 1

London UK April 1999

What's the point of editorial meetings? thought Julian, as he rushed out of his house, turning back briefly to retrieve his car keys that in haste he had almost forgotten. These occasions were always a pain and he approached this one with the same anathema that he had experienced for every other one since he joined the paper ten years previously. The situation was not helped by the decision of him and his wife to live in a town near the countryside outside of London, which worked for his day-to-day writing, but necessitated a train ride to the office for meetings such as this. An hour on a busy commuter train and tube from Sawbridgeworth seemed to exemplify in advance the misery that he knew he would experience at his destination. But at least his wife found it easier to get to work in Harlow, so, he told himself repeatedly, if she was happy, then so would he be.

His aversion to the forthcoming day, and the lack of motivation that accompanied it, had delayed his departure and, as usual, his expectations concerning the time taken to get to the station were over-optimistic. But he had done it: parked his car in a place that he knew would prompt a parking ticket, ran at full pelt into the station and leapt onto the train just as the doors were closing. Surprisingly, there were two adjacent empty seats - *backward-facing but never mind* - so he collapsed into the one by the aisle, head back, buttocks on the edge of the seat and legs extended straight in front. He closed his eyes and tried to regain control of his breathing. *Some people never learn*, he thought; *this happens every time. Luckily, no heart attacks so far - but one day?*

After a few minutes, when he had regained his composure, he began to make himself more comfortable for the journey ahead and sat up straight. As he shifted his rear back into the seat, he heard the jingling sound of coins falling from his trouser pocket. Inwardly cursing the bad trouser design, he turned in his seat to retrieve them but discovered that they had slipped down the side of the seat cushion. With difficulty because there was not much space, he forced his hand into the tiny gap. He could not quite reach the coins, which had come to lie underneath some paper seemingly trapped between the cushion and the seat. As he withdrew his hand, the paper slipped out with it.

It was an open envelope containing a letter. Instinctively, he withdrew the letter, unfolded it and began to read.

"Dear James,

I know you will not understand this, however much I try to explain it, but I have to leave. Nevertheless, to explain I will try. Before I do, however, it is sadly necessary for you to understand that you will never see me again. I am so unbelievably sorry about that but it is a fact. Do not, therefore, attempt to find me because you will not succeed. I really mean that - I do care for your future welfare but you would be best employed adapting to life without me because any alternative is impossible - absolutely impossible. Again I plead, do not try.

The reason I am leaving is nothing to do with you. I still love you now as I have always done - more so, in fact. But there are things that have been going on in my life and I am still suffering the consequences. I want you to know that I have done nothing wrong - really, truly - but there are people who I believe are determined to destroy me in as horrible a way as possible. I cannot explain more, partly because I do not fully understand myself, but I am not imagining this.

I would obviously have preferred to say all this to you in person but I had to leave in a hurry. I did not even have time to write a proper letter before I left, which is why I am posting this to you. I am so sorry but please believe me if there had been any other way out of this, I would have taken it willingly.

All my love,

Charlotte"

Instinctively, he picked up the envelope and examined the address: 9, Burlington Court, Hackney. In a moment, a rush of memories swept across his mind: *Hackney, Charlotte, James...a missing person.* Within a few minutes, the fragments had coalesced to one clear memory: he recalled vividly the article he wrote weeks earlier and the subsequent series of published comments, some by him and others by a series of experts, including psychiatrists and criminologists.

A girl named Charlotte, aged twenty-two, had suddenly and inexplicably disappeared from her home in Hackney. Very few of her personal belongings had been taken from the flat she shared with her boyfriend, James. There was no suicide note;

indeed, apart from a very brief, obscure parting letter to her boyfriend, there was no communication of any kind to indicate why and where she had gone. Her friends were unaware of any problems that she was experiencing and they all said that the relationship with her boyfriend of approaching one year's standing was unusually close. She seemed content in her clerical job in a large office and had given no notice, formal or informal, to her employers or work colleagues of her intention to leave. The police investigation was thorough but there was no evidence of break-in at the flat, no suspicious fingerprints and no other forensic clues.

Sadly, two days later, her boyfriend was hit by a train after having jumped from a bridge onto the railway track near to Cheshunt Station, on the line from London Liverpool Street. Now that he was permanently incapable of defending himself or providing any other kind of evidence, there was a brief spurt of gossip stemming from the fanciful imaginations of some of the locals. The most popular lay theory was that he had killed her, disposed of the body and then committed suicide. Although the police stressed that here was no evidence for that hypothesis, in some ways its appearance led to a form of closure in the community by a process of post-hoc rationalisation. The police kept the file open but the case generally went quiet.

On the way out, this line goes through Hackney on the way to Cambridge, thought Julian. *If these really are the same people, he must have taken this train from his home in Hackney with the letter on him and got off at Cheshunt, which he knew was one of the stations with a nearby bridge over the line. Gosh, he must have sat in this very seat!*

He rested his head back against the seat, closed his eyes and let his mind wander. He had been fascinated by the case when he first reported on it those weeks ago. He was never quite sure why but now wondered if some instinct told him then that there was a lot more to it than met the eye; now he was certain there was and he vowed to find out what.

Chapter 2

France 1880

As devout Roman Catholics, the family Bernard were regular attenders at mass on Sunday in their village of Saint Aignan in the French Loire Valley and worshipped at their own makeshift chapel in the family home every day without fail. The small vineyard had been within the family for several generations, producing Touraine wines, mostly sauvignon blanc and a cabernet red. The production was not large but the quality was high so the wines sold well and, despite its small size, the vineyard had kept viable. A steady return allowed the family to give regular donations to the church and still have just enough money left to maintain a simple but adequate lifestyle.

Over many years, as part of their faith, the family had held a longing desire to take a pilgrimage to The Sanctuary of Our Lady at Lourdes, a site deemed holy since a peasant girl, Bernadette Soubirous, received visions of the Virgin Mary there. Their yearning was particularly strong after their only child, Claudine, was born and it became clear, over the years, that the child was not strong. The poor girl was lethargic and slow to learn and could contribute little to the running of the vineyard, which required the full cooperation of the whole family. Her parents were convinced that contact with the Holy Mother would ease the child of the burdens that life had imposed upon her and Lourdes was the place where that contact was most likely to happen. Of course, their main concern was for the welfare of the child but a stronger daughter could also contribute more to the family's daily life and thereby add to its fulfilment and also that of the wider community, in keeping with God's wishes for His people on earth.

But the journey was one they could ill afford. Apart from horses, they had no means of travel and the cost of commissioning transport for a journey of some six hundred and fifty kilometres was prohibitive on their meagre income. Until, that is, a local benefactor, who had heard of their ambitions and took pity on the child, came to their aid. Robert Bonnaire, whose chateau had been in the family for many generations, was a lover of Touraine wines and particularly the highly individualistic ones of the Bernard vineyard. An unassuming man, despite his wealth, he was a regular visitor to the property where he would taste the recent vintages and buy quantities in person to lay down and mature in his own cellars. He had taken to the simple charm of the fourteen-year-old Claudine and the way in which her parents, particularly her mother, displayed a clear, constant concern for her welfare.

He had chosen not to intrude on the obvious anxiety that surrounded that relationship until, one day, his arrival was greeted by a mother in tears and her daughter struggling to climb onto a horse from a box, a task that would have proved simple for an average girl of her age, even without the assistance that Marie was providing to Claudine. The situation was so demanding of enquiry that Robert could not resist and she soon was recounting, sometimes in hurried speech, all the difficulties with life that her daughter had shown since her birth. They had been able to obtain advice only from limited local sources; any remedy proposed seemed powerless to help her. The only one who could now restore her to full health was the Holy Virgin

Mary and Marie knew that the Mother of God would create that miracle if only Claudine could be taken to meet her at Lourdes.

Robert was not only a sympathetic man; he also held a strong Catholic faith and, whilst he did not share the absolute conviction of the universal healing power of the sanctuary at Lourdes (many people had visited without receiving any overwhelming spiritual experience), he knew that what Marie hoped for from a visit there was at least possible. He invited the family to his chateau to discuss ways forward.

The family had never seen anything so grand so close. As the carriage provided by Robert carried them up the drive, they craned their heads out of the side windows, scarcely able to absorb, in the time available, the symmetrical centre of the building with its arched main door, the dome-topped towers to the side and the formal gardens that seemed to extend further than they could see and punctuated by majestic statues. Even Claudine, who had spent most of the journey quiet and slunk back in her chair, began to jump about the interior of the carriage bumping frequently, in the confined space, against the knees of her parents and squealing randomly. In the distance were the chateau's own vineyards; why then, asked Marie was Monsieur Bonnaire so interested in their wines? Because he liked them, he later explained.

Inside the building, their wonder was no less. The walls of the reception room were lined with mirrors, which Claudine used in turn to study herself from as many angles as possible until she was persuaded to sit on one of the red velvet-covered chairs next to a large, circular, mahogany table.

Robert had made a decision and took no time to tell them. Even though their attention remained distracted by the splendour of the surroundings in which they found themselves, they did not miss the crucial pronouncement of their host: that he was prepared not only to fund their visit to Lourdes but also to provide the carriages, attendants and anything else that they would need for the journey. In particular, he would discharge one of his housemaids, Colette Girard, from her regular duties so that she could accompany the family and give special attention to Claudine on the journey and in her quest to confront the Virgin Mary. Colette was chosen, he explained, because she was a woman of more mature years whose whole family had worked at the chateau; Robert knew her well and she had shown particular empathy towards his own children as they were growing up. He explained that he had already spoken to her and she was, of course, not only willing to carry out any duties required of her by her master but was positively excited by the specific task that he had chosen for her.

And a kindly woman she did indeed appear to be. Her first gesture, after he brought her into the room and following the formal introductions, was to take hold of Claudine's hands, bend forward and smile broadly deep into her face. Claudine, for her part, returned the smile and was visibly calm. Marie looked at them both with an air of deep satisfaction and optimism.

The journey would be made by horse and carriage. Robert considered use of the newly flourishing rail system in France but decided it was still too unreliable; the connections would be numerous and parts of the journey would not be covered by any rail service so some other means of transport would have to be used to cover those. He was also something of a traditionalist at heart. Rightly or wrongly, he decided that up to a month's journey by carriage could easily take just as long by rail. The venues for overnight stays and care and replacement of the horses would all be made in advance through his extensive network of influential contacts. He promised to the family that he would take care of it all and let them know when the plans had been completed. He also assured them that the necessary work on their vineyard would be covered in their absence by his own staff. Marie felt that half of the miracle that she was looking for had already been fulfilled. Claudine understood that she was to embark on a long journey, something she had never done before, and was filled with excitement. Collette smiled unceasingly.

The whole family was still buoyant by the time their journey began, some three to four weeks later. Even from within the confines of their carriage, their minds were flooded with new visions of the French towns and countryside, sometimes reassuringly similar to the area around their home village and sometimes excitedly different. But the journey was also wearing and, by several days from the start, Claudine had taken to spending long periods asleep in the carriage. Her mother had tried to maintain her attention by pointing out every new sighting along the way but that in itself proved mentally taxing and added to her daughter's somnolence. As a result, when she should have been able to sleep properly, overnight at one of the coaching inns, Claudine slept fitfully and dreamt a lot. Often, she would recount the details of her dreams to her parents and Colette over *le petit déjeuner* the following morning: the dogs jumping about in the undergrowth by the roadside as they passed in their carriage; bright orange birds talking to her from the branches of the trees in a language that she could not understand (it wasn't French, she added by way of clarification); travelling sometimes in a very fast coach with the horses at a gallop towards the distant horizon that never seemed to get closer. Although behaviour not typical of Claudine, who at home slept every night without disturbance, her stories, obviously the outpourings of an excited mind, only added to the family sense of fulfilment that the generosity of Monsieur Bonnaire had bestowed upon them.

Fellow travellers along the way shared in their joy. A teenage girl was not a frequent visitor to the residential inns of the main routes so her presence in itself was a novelty, a source of interest for those for whom travelling was a way of life and not a very exciting one at that. The lame horses, the hills where people would have to dismount from the heavy carriage to enable the struggling horses to pull it to the top, the uneven roads often disfigured by the hooves of cattle, the boredom and the sometimes demanding passengers taxed their stamina. And Claudine's outgoing honesty, unrestrained by convention, had particular appeal. So it was that often, at many of their stays along their journey, the Bernards mixed with travelling men and by extension many of their female passengers, who were more keen than usual to engage in conversation and enquire with genuine interest the purpose of their travels. So removed from the simplicity of their rural, isolated life in their vineyard in Saint Aignan, the family, especially Marie, began to bask in their unprompted attention and feel some special worth. The optimism felt at the start of their venture developed into a committed certainty towards their goal.

But, approaching three weeks into their journey, the fatigue began to tell. Claudine's disturbed nights and catnapping through the day began to cloud her mind. Unusually for her, she began to show bouts of unprompted irritability. When it was directed towards her parents, they were usually able to accommodate it because they had spent the whole of their daughter's lifetime dealing with her difficulties, albeit of a different type. One of them, usually her mother, did not attempt to respond in kind but simply held her close, speaking soft words, until Claudine settled and often went to sleep.

But when Claudine challenged Colette, it was different. Colette believed that, in the short but close time together, she had formed a particularly close bond with the child and reacted to her rebuttals with hurt and a feeling of being unfairly challenged. Unlike Claudine's parents, who reacted emotionally, she attempted to rationalise the child's behaviour from the words she said and, finding no good explanation, reacted with personal affront. No doubt the fatigue that she too was experiencing reduced her tolerance and ability to see the situation as her parents did - the inexplicable rantings of a very tired child.

But she did not rise; her response was usually to become silent, one which unfortunately all too often provoked Claudine's wrath even more. As the journey progressed, Colette's feelings of redundancy and rejection increased until she chose to adopt an air of isolation and spent most of the time impassive and uncommunicative in the carriage. Did she brood? Most certainly; her master had furnished her with a special role, the guardian of a vulnerable child and now her charge had risen up in rebellion against her, sapping her sense of position and responsibility. At the chateau, she was valued day after day; her role was secure and stable; she felt important and integral to the smooth running of the household. Now she was reduced to little more than worthless, all because of the will of a child, whose behaviour would never have been tolerated in the high moral echelons of the chateau. Colette harboured a brewing resentment.

As they were heading towards Montaubon, Claudine's attention was caught by a disturbance ahead, amongst some reed beds not far from the road. As she watched more closely, she saw a large, dark grey bird with a chestnut-red head and breast furtively wading amongst them.

"Look, look!" she said. "Look at that! It's a bird, a very big bird!"

"That's a heron," said Marie. "Isn't it magnificent? Such grace!" Colette, looking towards the reed beds, raised her hand to her forehead to shield her eyes from the sun reflecting from the water. As the carriage approached more closely, the rattling of the coach wheels disturbed the bird, which waded further into the depth of the reeds, out of sight.

"You did that!" shouted Claudine to Colette. "With your hand, you frightened it away. You did it on purpose. I saw you!"

"Nonsense, Claudine," said Colette. "It wasn't me; it was the noise of our carriage as it approached."

"I saw you! You waved your hand and then my friend, the bird, ran away." Colette said nothing more and turned to face the side window. Claudine's mother put her arm around her daughter and pulled her lovingly towards her but Claudine pulled away.

"She did it because that bird was my friend. All she had to do was lift up her hand to send a message to him and he ran away. She did it because she does not like me."

"I think Colette likes you very much and we are honoured to have her with us."

"I did like you very much," said Colette, turning back towards the child, albeit with indifference. "But you are making it very difficult because you persist in saying things about me that are not true. And it is very hurtful. I cannot take that. Please stop so maybe we can enjoy our time together again, as indeed we did so much when we started off." She turned her head to look out to the countryside.

"You do not like me and you want something to happen to me so I would then be out of your way!" Her mother tried again to hold her and this time Claudine did not resist. She settled into her mother's arms.

"Once we get to Lourdes, you will find that everything will be all right; I promise you," whispered Marie into her ear. Claudine slept. Colette remained silent.

Their inn for the night was on the approach to Montaubon. By the time of their arrival, the child had woken, refreshed from her sleep, and renewed with energy. André Bernard had told his wife to keep their daughter awake so that she would sleep well that night but Marie implored him to let her sleep, not least for the comfort of their aide, Colette, and he acquiesced.

As expected, Claudine slept erratically, dreaming often. On this occasion, however, the content of her dreams changed from the previous benign fantasies that so often amused her fellow travellers when she recounted them the following morning to something more dire. For the first half of the night, she was

16

woken virtually hourly by nightmares of insects crawling around the walls and dark creatures, half humanoid and half with the shape of goats, bulls and horses that moved slowly towards her bedside, seemingly increasing in size as they did so. Each time, Claudine sat up abruptly, shaking and sweating. The sound of her cries drew her mother rapidly to her side and, with her now practised comforting methods, Marie was, after ten or fifteen minutes, able to return her daughter to sleep. Until the next time.

On the fifth wakening, Claudine would not be comforted and she pushed her mother away. Unlike before, she could no longer recognise the abhorrent images as part of a dream because she insisted that they were still present and she pointed across the room.

"They are there; can you not see them? Look!"

"Claudine, what do you think you can see? Tell me for I promise there is nothing there."

"There!" said her daughter pointing repeatedly. "That black thing. And another beside it. Look, it's coming to get me!" She buried her head under the rudimentary bedcovers.

"Come out, Claudine," said her mother, lifting back the covers. "Look, look hard, there's nothing there." But the child was insistent, insistent until finally the fatigue again overcame her and she fell back, breathing heavily, and lapsed into a deep sleep that continued for the rest of the night.

The next day, they were back on the road again and Claudine seemed more settled albeit tired and quiet. Just over two hours into their journey, the weather was good and the passengers and assistants decided to stop the carriage and step out for a short break. In general, the closer they got to Lourdes, the more they saw other travellers, pilgrims like them en route to the same destination. When they saw another coach stationary by the side of the road, the Bernard group stopped, sensing that the men and ladies ambling along the field edge nearby shared a common interest, but they placed their carriage a respectable distance away and walked gently towards them, not wishing to be intrusive. Fortunately, the strangers seemed receptive and, after formal introductions by the men, freely engaged in conversation, confirming that their goal was also to receive a holy blessing at The Sanctuary of Our Lady.

Initially, Claudine had remained in the coach but, after a few minutes, was seen by one of the group running towards them.

"Is this child one of yours?" enquired one of the ladies of Colette.

"No," said Marie before Colette could answer, "she is my daughter."

"She seems a charming child," said the stranger, as Claudine reached the group.

The lady, Madame Beaufort, smiled at Claudine and then returned to conversation with the others.

"I saw ghosts!" said Claudine suddenly and unprompted.

"Ghosts?" said Madame, wide-eyed.

"Claudine," said her mother, taking her by the arm and pulling her to one side, "enough of this! These ladies whom we have just met do not want to hear of your wild fantasies."

"No, it's all right," said Madame. "Please, do tell us."

"I saw ghosts! Last night, there were three of them, big and black. They had hands like people but heads of animals; one was a goat."

Madame Beaufort seemed more interested in this seemingly nonsensical utterance of a child than one might expect. She prompted Claudine to tell more and soon learnt that the creatures were indeed threatening and, no, they did not seem as if their intentions were good. But they had offered Claudine magic towels to keep her healthy, as long as she promised to be friends with them.

"Interesting, but I have to say very worrying," said Madame, stroking the silver cross that hung around her neck and staring sternly towards the child with the air of a priest.

Without the necessary words being said, Marie nevertheless sensed the implications of the lady's pronouncement and actions. A strong feeling of holy disapproval was made manifest. In despair, she turned towards her daughter. "Claudine," said Marie, "what is this? There were no ghosts. I was with you, remember, and I assure you there were none. And last night you said nothing about any magic towels and I was with you until you went back to sleep. You have either made up all this story about towels or your fantasies are now running even more wild."

"The ghosts came back after you had left," said Claudine, with no emotion.

The pilgrims en route to Lourdes often had a heightened sense of the spiritual for that was, after all, the goal of their mission and Madame Beaufort was certainly one of them. Her mind had become increasingly focussed on the conflict between good and evil the closer she became to her destination; more and more, she consciously analysed the world around her as she passed through the countryside - the trees, the birds, the carcasses of dead animals by the side of the road and, of course, the behaviour and conversations of her fellow travellers. She had spent much of the latter part of the journey in prayer. So it was perhaps not surprising that she had taken a keen interest in the seemingly malevolent content of Claudine's experiences.

"Do you still have the towels?" she asked the child.

"Yes, I'll go and get them." But her mother held her back and refused to let her leave her side, sensing the disquiet in her new-found companion.

"Madame, these are the imaginings of a child," she said, in a raised voice. "My daughter is loving, charming and honest but she is not strong, which is the main reason for our travel to the Holy Sanctuary, to seek the blessing of our Holy Mother in making her sound in body - and also in mind. I urge you not to take seriously the things that she reports. They are truly fantasies." Marie was shaking and close to tears.

"Possibly," said Madame Beaufort. She turned away from Marie to resume conversation with the others.

"Colette," cried Marie, "tell them what you know, I implore you. Tell them that you know my daughter and she is as innocent as the wind." Colette stood rigid and remained silent.

André Bernard ushered his family back to the coach. A loving and caring husband and father, he was nevertheless a distant person who seldom exposed his thoughts or feelings. His position, he thought, as head of the household should carry sufficient weight and authority by virtue of its very nature; his direction for his family in life should be clear without his having to recount it and his reaction to the ups and downs of life should be obvious. Yes, in day-to-day life, he would give instructions or discuss practical matters because he had to but never in any depth. In general, he assumed that his wife would interpret and act on the events that befell them in accordance with his wishes and feelings with no need for his personal intervention. Indeed, he never questioned that she had not done so. Thus he was overall the quiet man. For Marie, however, things were not that clear. She accepted, of course, his dominant position in the family and did her best to accommodate his will in the actions that she took each day. But that will, and the reason and emotion that underlay it, were not as obvious to her as he imagined they would be. And she had her own feelings, which she could not ignore. Just occasionally, maybe, he could voice his deeper thoughts, she hoped, but she knew it would not happen, at least with any substance, and so all she could do was the best as she saw it.

They resumed their journey; Marie held her arm around her daughter; André and Colette sat silent. In the other coach, Madame Beaufort sat in prayer for the first ten minutes after they had set off, then sat upright and stared into the distance pensively. After a further few minutes, she turned to her companion.

"Thérèse, I have been thinking in depth about that young girl we met when we stopped for a rest and the experiences that she recounted to us. What is your opinion?"

"I have too, Joséphine. She certainly made an impression on me and I could see that she did on you too. I have to say it all sounds very strange. It is not, I would consider, to be the sort of dream that most young girls would have and I wonder if she is a little disturbed. Her mother did allude to seeking blessing at the Sanctuary to ease her daughter's ills."

"It is more than that, I believe. The beings that visited her - dark forms, half human and half goat - those are typical of what we understand of Satan's messengers. I have tried not to think this way but I cannot avoid it. I fear that she has been visited by the Devil."

"But her mother saw nothing."

"The Evil One is selective in his visitations. He is quite capable of making himself known to one person whilst being invisible to another."

"But then we must pray for her."

"Indeed we must. I just hope - and pray - that she has not acquiesced to his demands. But I admit on that account I worry. She talked of being offered towels by the demons in return for friendship. My heartfelt concern is that she agreed because she spoke of still having the towels; indeed she offered to show them to us and would have done so if her mother had not prevented her."

"If you are right in your thoughts on this, Joséphine, what does that mean for the child, do you believe?"

"If she has done a deal with the servants of Satan, then she has become one of his followers. There is no escaping that. And her fate is irreversible, save for intervention by the grace of God. But she would need to ask for His forgiveness before that could happen. If she does not, she is bound to the pursuit of evil."

"We can pray that she will do that."

"Indeed we can." And they bowed their heads in prayer.

Approximately fifty kilometres from Lourdes, the Bernard coach driver decided to stop to provide another rest period for the passengers and horses. A pleasant spot, he decided, would be by a river in the distance, bordered by plane trees, which might provide shade from the full sun. There they would be able to take some refreshment in preparation for the next stage of the journey. As they approached, Marie saw another coach stationary by the riverside. Still raw from her previous encounter with strangers, she urged the driver not to approach too closely; whilst consciously realising that the chances of a similar experience with a new set of acquaintances was very small, her emotions would not let her take the risk and she urged the others not to approach them. Dismounting from the coach, they settled on the grass of the riverbank under the branches of one of the trees and took the opportunity to relax by simply watching the turbulence of the fast-flowing river as the water coursed around the large stones on the river bed. Even Claudine seemed mesmerised by the motion.

But their peace and solitude did not last. From behind came the sound of a woman's voice. Marie's anxiety at having to talk to more strangers was compounded dramatically when she turned and discovered who was addressing them: Madame Beaufort.

"Well, hello again!" said Madame with exaggerated pleasantness.

Contrary to his usual nature, André Bernard decided that only he could prevent a recurrence of the confrontation that had so much upset his wife on the previous occasion. He stood and walked purposefully towards Joséphine Beaufort although, by now, she was only a few metres from the entire group.

"Hello, Madame. I trust you are well and tolerating this hard journey to our Holy Shrine."

But André's new-found boldness had little influence on a robust and determined lady, such as Madame Beaufort. His attempts to check her forward movement were quickly dispelled as, albeit with grace, she side-stepped him and walked on.

"Very well, thank you, sir. And how is the rest of the family? Claudine, you seem so much calmer than last time we met, if you will permit me to say so. Perhaps the journey has tired you. But do not worry; we will soon reach our destination. And may I assume from your present demeanour that you have not witnessed any more of those frightening beings that you related to us on the last occasion of our meeting. I do very much hope so for I know how demanding they can be."

Claudine stood and acknowledged her guest with the politeness she had been taught but then remained silent and, when her mother stood, turned back towards the river and resumed her gazing at the water.

"Hello again, Madame," said Marie. "Rest assured my daughter has now recovered from the bad dreams that so disturbed her and I am pleased to relate that they have not recurred. I have no doubt that the trials of the journey had upset her, particularly with deprived or erratic sleep, but now she has become accustomed to it, her mind has become more settled. And, as you so wisely point out, that journey is almost at an end so we can all be truly comforted that she will suffer no further distress."

By now, two of Madame Beaufort's fellow travellers had joined her and the three stood defiantly facing the Bernards. An atmosphere had certainly descended upon the group, which was clear to all, but each one endeavoured to maintain an air of respect and politeness, notwithstanding that they all harboured determined, if different, motives. Marie was, of course, set on protecting her daughter. The whole point of their pilgrimage, to provide healing to her sickly Claudine, would be potentially lost if this stranger succeeded in persecuting the child for some intangible reason. *I know how demanding these beings can be. What exactly did she mean by that?* André was, as usual, practical and fundamentalist in his thoughts; his goal was for this rather intrusive stranger simply to leave them alone and go her own way so that they could go theirs and he hoped that by just waiting patiently she would eventually give up her rather tiresome discourse. Madame Beaufort, however, was not one to let evil flourish and where she saw that Satan may be in action, her faith would not allow her to ignore it for to do so would be denying God's work - and therefore also hers - here on earth. Colette and Claudine had managed to resume some of their earlier closeness so care of the child was foremost in her thoughts. Colette sat close to her, sharing her impressions of the water bubbling over the rocks, but saying nothing.

"Well, horrible dreams they certainly were," said Madame Beaufort, "if indeed that is the correct interpretation of your daughter's experiences. If you will forgive me, I would not wish to let it pass that some other force might have been at work to cause such distress to your daughter, at least initially."

Marie felt her anxiety mounting once again and with it an increasing boldness.

"Of what exactly do you speak, Madame?"

"I speak of the form of the creatures that Claudine described: black, half human and half goat. With your mission to visit the Holy Shrine of the Virgin Mary, I must assume that you are aware of the significance of that form of creature. And they gave your daughter gifts did they not?"

"Gifts?"

"Towels, I believe."

Marie tried hard to suppress the sudden sensation of exploding anger. But she did not need to do because Claudine herself dramatically altered the atmosphere.

"They came back again. Last night, they came back again," she said without shifting her gaze from the river. Marie's impending outburst was stifled in an instant. Madame Beaufort's expression changed to a cold stare directed towards the back of the child's head. One of her companions closed her eyes, turned her head upwards and formed the sign of the cross with one hand, forehead to low chest, left shoulder to right. Marie tried hard through her panic to rationalise. *Claudine slept soundly, there were no bad dreams, I would have known. Yes, I slept but I would have woken. If she had been frightened, I would have known, I would have woken. And the towels - what towels? She has no towels yet she says she has. My poor daughter, she is so poorly now, I must get her to the Shrine.*

"My daughter was sleeping next to me," she said calmly, "and, if she had been disturbed by bad dreams, I can assure you, Madame, that I would have woken. And I did not."

"Indeed, Madame," said Madame Beaufort, "I am sure that, had your daughter been frightened or disturbed, you would have woken, as you indicate. But you did not waken. That shows that the visit from the beings did not distress her. And the reason is that she has befriended them. That is why they gave her the towels - because she agreed to be one of their agents. You may find it hard to face up to, Madame, but that is the case."

"Madame Beaufort," said André calmly, "you are making assumptions that in truth have no foundation. Our daughter is a sickly child and is prone to imaginings. It is no more than that and I implore you to take it as such."

"Sir, I assure you that I am concerned for your child but I have spent much of my life studying the ways of the Evil One and, in God's name, seeking to eradicate his influence in this world. Your daughter can still be freed from his grasp but she will need to ask for God's forgiveness for what she has done in colluding with his agents. And that is what they are - his agents - the black, half-human, half-goat that appears in the night and offers rewards for friendship is the typical manifestation of one of his followers. We must now beseech your daughter to seek God's forgiveness in order to be freed from her enslavement. God is merciful and will release her. But she must ask."

Marie screamed. "What are you suggesting? Are you saying that my daughter is a witch?"

Joséphine Beaufort's companion crossed herself again. "It is sad to relate, Madame, but that is what she has made herself."

Marie ran to her daughter. "Tell them, Claudine, that you have made up this story before they do you harm. Tell them, if you cannot do that, that you have not made friends with these creatures that you see - and that only you see."

"They are there, Maman, and they speak to me. They told me that they would not harm me if I agreed to be their friend. They gave me the towels as a reward when I said I would and they went away. When they came back, they were much nicer. I don't want people to hurt me. It frightens me when I think someone might hurt me."

"Just as I told you," said Madame Beaufort. She walked purposefully towards Claudine, who stood to face her and began breathing heavily.

"Do not hurt her!" shouted Marie, taking hold of the lady's arm and attempting to hold her back. Colette remained immobile and silent, standing by the side of the river.

"I will not hurt the child. I simply want her to save herself from the powers of the Evil One. I want her to pray to the Lord for forgiveness and release from the clutches into which she has placed herself. Come, my child; let us pray."

During the time that the group had been at the riverside, the bright sunlight had gradually faded but, as Madame spoke, that dullness was superimposed by an unusual darkness that began to move over the area. The attention of the group was stilled. They looked to the sky through half-closed eyes to see a large section of the sun cut out, leaving a small residual crescent of bright light. As the crescent grew yet smaller, wavy lines of alternate light and dark began to move across the ground around them. They continued to watch in awe and mounting fear as the remaining tiny portion of the sun gradually disappeared to leave just a small ball of light to one side and a narrow ring of light around its body, a diamond ring in the sky. The jewel then faded to be replaced by tiny blobs of light around the black disc, which slowly developed a reddish hue. In mounting incomprehension, their wide eyes scanned alternately between the weaving pattern on the earth and the changes moving around the sun.

Soon the earth was plunged into total darkness; the birds stopped singing; and the total eclipse was complete. But none of those present knew of eclipses, let alone having seen one; the reaction was of terror. Except, that is, for Claudine who, apparently unmoved, had turned her gaze back towards the now blackened waves of the flowing river.

"Our sun is dissolving," said Françoise, trembling. "Our sun is dissolving." Madame Beaufort's associate stood transfixed, gazing open-mouthed towards the sky. Then her eyes flitted from one to another of the other women. "It's going," she said, her voice in mounting agitation. "We are losing the sun!"

"This is just the sort of thing I feared," said Madame Beaufort, now standing rigid and immobile, "but even I never imagined her actions could be so vile. My friends, greet evil in its full confrontation. If you ever had doubts about the power of the Devil and his agents, dispel them now for they are showing themselves in their full dark glory. Do you notice the reactions of those here present? You, my partners in faith, and the whole of the family we have come to know, show bodily reactions that no reasonable person could interpret as anything but fear and incomprehension. Look at them - they tremble! Except, that is, for one. Do you see her, even in the darkness, sitting by the riverside, unmoved by what is going on around her? Does this not confirm what we have been saying since we heard the girl talk about her communications with the messengers of The Dark One?"

"Do you mean she has caused all this?" said another, crying. "Is she bringing about the end of the world?"

"Look at it all," said Madame. "Open your eyes through the blackness and you will see there is little doubt. We find ourselves amongst the most threatening power to our God here on earth in recent times."

"What can be done?" said Françoise.

"Only she has the way out of it for all of us. She is not yet totally resigned to the Evil One. By reassigning her will to that of Our Lord, the dark powers will ebb away and she and us will be saved from destruction. We have to give her absolution but she has to receive it willingly. Come, let us approach her." The group of three women moved in determined unison towards Claudine at the river bank.

But Claudine looked up and perceived a threatening demeanour in the women as they walked. She stood. In the darkness, all she could sense were dark shapes moving purposefully towards her, with malicious intent. As Madame approached, Claudine backed away in fear. Undaunted, Madame quickened her pace, her expression now resolute with intent. Her two associates joined her in pursuit, effectively trapping the child between them and the river. But Claudine, with increasing alarm, began to run away from the three towards the river, her head half-turned back to judge, as far as she could, the progress of her pursuers. Marie screamed in panic. Colette stood by watching, unmoved.

And then it was too late for prayer, redemption or anything else that might have brought down the curtain on this sorry enactment. For, with her head still turned, and in just a glimmer of light, Claudine was unable to see clearly where her legs were taking her; she stumbled on a rocky outgrowth close to the river bank. One leg bent beneath her; her body turned and she fell backwards into the water. The sound of her head striking a stone protruding from the river was audible to all and then she was gone, her body disappearing beneath the surface of the fast-moving current.

Within minutes, light shone bright again and the sun returned.

Chapter 3

New Amboise, Illinois, USA   September 1948

Annie awoke with a start, alerted by a rustling sound outside her ground-floor bedroom window. As she jumped from her bed, the noise increased in intensity but then started to fade, as if someone who had been lurking had begun to run away. When she looked through the window, she sensed a dark silhouette of a person moving in a direction directly away from the bungalow. The night was dark and her vision was distorted by the vertical sheets of rain but she sensed the figure was clad in a long coat and a tight-fitting cap. At that point, her nostrils became filled by an acrid odour which persisted despite her moving away from the window and instead gradually increased in intensity however she tried to escape it, even after leaving the bedroom. A sense of panic overcame her.

Within a few minutes, her eyes began to burn and stream and she started to cough and retch. Feeling suddenly faint, she returned to bed but the symptoms did not abate. Despite her distress, she tried hard to identify the nature of the smell, not least so that she could hopefully locate it and eradicate it. Her first inclination was that a gas leak had developed within the house but she soon concluded that the smell was quite different from that of domestic gas. Although pungent, this was much sweeter, like some sort of fragranced acid.

As the faintness seemed to ease a little, she decided to get up and investigate but, although she could move her arms well enough, her legs seemed heavy and lifeless. She swayed her upper body from side to side in an attempt to mobilise them but they felt as if stuck to the mattress beneath. With the realisation that half of her body was paralysed came mounting panic. Her heart raced; she began to sweat; the nausea increased and the faintness returned. She collapsed backwards in a state of overwhelming powerlessness.

That was her last memory until she regained awareness about two hours later. Before anything else, and with great trepidation, she took a deep breath through her nostrils; the smell had gone. Gingerly, she tried to move one leg to the side of the bed; it moved. With increasing confidence, she tried the other; it moved. *Thank God*, she said to herself and gave a long, low sigh.

Aided by intense mental fatigue, she slept albeit fitfully until her father returned from his night shift around seven a.m. Frankly, he thought, his daughter's account did not really make sense, especially since he knew she was something of a fantasist, but her reaction to his scepticism shocked him into listening more closely. So adamant was she that it was not a dream, the odour and sound of some passing nocturnal animal or any other rational explanation that he could offer that he was surprised to find that he inclined to believe her. Yet he always prided himself on being a sensible and guiding parent and half of his mind continued to search for some everyday happening that, in an instant, would dispel her anxieties and now, to some extent, his too.

But he could not explain everything. The most rational part of her account and, as far as their future safety was concerned, was the prowler. For that reason alone, he decided, the police would have to be informed - and perhaps, if he could persuade his daughter to keep quiet, their case would not be undermined by the details that were harder to believe.

"Let me do the talking," Joseph said to her as they approached the police station. "It's only that I know you are very upset and I don't want to make it worse by you having to go through all the details again. I'll tell them about the prowler but they do not need to know the rest. All we need to do is get him caught and then we can all rest in our beds - literally."

"But he tried to poison me! Don't you think it's important that the police know that? Because I do!"

"If it turns out that it's something they need to know to catch this guy, then we'll tell them, ok? But let's just take it one step at a time."

"Dad, you didn't have to go through what I went through. I was nearly choked and I was paralysed! He might end up killing someone!"

"Well, not if he's caught, he won't, will he? Don't worry, honey; we'll get this guy off the streets once and for all."

The interview seemed to go well, Jo declared afterwards and the news that a prowler had been reported by someone else in the area the same night meant that the case was taken very seriously by the police without his having to give too much detail, which, in his own mind he thought, they would find hard to believe. Jo had had time to reflect on his daughter's experiences over the few hours between his arrival home and their visit to the police and, yes, she was certainly convincing but, as he thought about it, more questions seemed to be posed than were answered. He was no expert, that he knew, but why would someone want to poison people in their beds without trying to burgle them afterwards, he thought? Are there poisons that can half paralyse someone for just a few hours? *Maybe, I suppose.*

Two days later, Jo came down to breakfast, looking forward to the first of his weekend days off work. Even though now barely fifteen years old, Annie had had to mature quickly following the death of her mother two years earlier. Her father had had to continue to go out to work to keep the two of them afloat and she had willingly taken on the role of

housekeeper, a task that became much easier after she dropped out of school.

He came through the kitchen door to find her, as usual around that time of day, busy at the stove, cooking the eggs, with her back towards him. As he helped himself to coffee from the pot on the range, she responded to his breezy "Hi, great day" not with her usual everyday patter but a more sombre "Seen the paper?"

"Thought I'd take a look over breakfast," said Jo.

"Take a look now."

Jo ambled over to the kitchen table where the newspaper was laid, the front page up towards him. "Wow!" he said, after a moment's glance.

Gassing Prowler on the Loose

A thirteen-year-old suffered a terrifying experience Thursday night when she was nearly killed by a mystery poisoner. The girl was woken from her sleep coughing and sneezing, seemingly caused by some sort of gas that a prowler let loose through her bedroom window. Despite streaming eyes, the unfortunate girl was just able to see the outline of someone running away from the house, wearing a long coat and a tight fitting hat. Needless to say, the attack has caused great distress to her and her parents. Police have been alerted and have launched a major enquiry but, until the perpetrator of this cowardly act has been brought to justice, residents are advised to take all possible precautions, including ensuring that doors are locked and windows are kept firmly closed. Anyone with any information should contact the police at the earliest opportunity.

"Now do you think we should have told the police everything about what happened to me?" said Annie.

Jo fell silent; then, after a few minutes' reflection, replied,"Well, possibly, but, in one sense, we didn't need to because they know now anyway."

"Dad, they need all the evidence they can get to capture this maniac! Why do you seem to want to dismiss all the horrible things I went through? It comes across as if you don't believe me. Well, anyway, whether you did or not, perhaps you will now that it's obvious that he's carrying on with his murderous mission and it's splashed all over the newspapers."

Jo didn't need to say much more; in fact, there was not a lot he could say, he reflected, because his daughter was obviously correct. After a few minutes, he said simply: "We'll go back and tell them everything."

"Thank you."

George and Walter picked up their beers from the bar and settled down at one of the simple wooden tables by the window. The setting of the sun behind the warehouse on the far side of the street had already cast a dark shadow across the buildings on the near side; soon the town would be plunged into another black night, any moonlight or starlight obscured by a heavy overcast layer of clouds.

Walter stared through the window at the impending gloom and what it may bring.

"What do you make of all this prowler business - with the gassings and all?" he asked his companion.

"Well, it's not something we're used to in this sleepy old town," said George. "The most exciting thing that happened before that was when Jon Garcia lost eight sheep in one night from some mystery predator, about eight years ago. Remember that? Mind you, it shows how short of excitement the folks are here because that 'mystery predator' was a talking point for weeks when anyone with any sense would guess pretty straight off that it was likely one of a number of things that live around here - bear, bobcat, wolf, lion - you name it. But I guess that's too easy!" They both laughed, then took a gulp of beer in synchrony.

"No," said Walter, putting down his glass, "we should be serious. You have to admit that this is something different. It's not that it's just one crazy person imagining things; there have been five of them to date and it seems unlikely that they are all off their heads at the same time. After all, we haven't had a full moon or anything like that recently."

They laughed again. "It can't be someone from round here," said George, "because we know all of these folks - have done for years. Well, not unless one of them has suddenly lost their mind and turned into a would-be murderer, which I suppose is possible. Either that or it's someone from outside the area."

"Or someone who has moved here recently," said Walter. "We're not going to know them are we - exactly because they have just come so no-one will know them well."

"That's pretty obvious," said George.

"Thanks!" said his companion. "Then why didn't you think of it?" They laughed again and took another gulp of beer.

It was later than intended when Walter set off for home and he had one or two more beers than intended inside him. By now, around nine-thirty, the area was in near total darkness. The main thoroughfare was clear enough from the street lighting but the side streets, which Walter would have to take to reach home, had no such benefit. Fortunately, he had trodden this route many times in the dark and felt that, by now, he could probably do it with his eyes closed. Some relief was also provided from time to time by the light from the occasional house along the back streets, at least those whose blinds had been left open.

As he reached the end of the first side street of the main road, he turned left opposite the outdoor clothes store and headed towards the crossroads where a right turn would take him into even smaller and more dimly lit streets. Visibility was poor but the bar on the corner as usual provided some welcome light. As he prepared to turn right, he glanced down the road ahead running next to the bar where numerous side alleys led to a network of small timber houses hidden from the main part of town. Then he sensed movement.

His awareness of danger heightened by the conversation earlier in the evening, he stopped, narrowed his eyes and stared down the road ahead. Unmistakably was the outline of a person half walking and half running away from where he stood. He stared harder, hoping to glean some information that might help to identify the man that had instilled fear into a community previously so peaceful. So seldom did he usually see anyone on these streets in the dark that he felt confident that this person ahead was he. Maybe his observations would make all the difference in finding him. Then he managed to identify a close fitting, probably woollen cap, a jacket tucked at the waist - and a calf-length loose skirt. A woman! He began to follow her but soon after she took one of the side roads which, with the available light, Walter could not identify precisely. He ran down the road ahead, gazing down each of the alleys, but the light was too poor to see much beyond the first few yards of each. He finally admitted to himself that she had disappeared; he turned round and, deep in thought, resumed his familiar route home.

Involuntarily, he glanced over his shoulder before he put the key in the door, closed it with unusual haste and quickly turned on the hall light. He went straight to the kitchen, took a beer from the fridge and wrenched off the cap. *Probably a bad idea*, he thought, *but what the hell?* He slumped into his favourite chair in the lounge, gave a long sigh and gazed through the window into a sea of blackness.

The following morning, Walter prepared himself to go down to the police station to do what he considered to be his duty but he was not relishing the prospect. It seemed to him that the police were so intent on believing that this neighbourhood was the best in the United States that anyone trying to allege anything to the contrary was themselves immediately suspect. At least, that was his experience two years earlier when he reported seeing someone steal a bicycle from outside the grocery store. Are you sure it wasn't his? Could he have been borrowing it? Even Walter's statement that a man came running out of the store shouting that someone had stolen his bike did not seem to produce much effect. All they wanted to know was what Walter was doing in the area. Still, this gassing business seemed so serious that he knew he had to report anything that was unusual and could be relevant so off he went.

"Thank you, sir," said the police officer, "and did you get a good view, do you have a good description of this woman?"

"Not really, Officer. As I have said, it was pretty dark out there but I did manage to see that she was wearing a tight cap, a short jacket and a long skirt. I would say that she was about five foot eight."

"Hmm. Well, that could apply to any one of a number of women in this town. Anything else?"

"I know that route well and you seldom see anyone out in those streets after dark, especially not scurrying around suspiciously. I thought it odd and, with all this prowler business going on recently, I felt you should know. At least I can be confident it was a woman."

"You do know from newspaper reports, I guess, that other observers have felt that the perpetrator was a man?"

"Yes, Officer," said Walter with a barely disguised sigh.

"Do you think you would recognise her if you saw her again?"

"Possibly, if she was wearing the same clothes, but I guess not otherwise."

"Well, she's not going to go around dressed so she knows she could be recognised again, is she, Mr. Michaels?"

"No, Officer." *There again! Why am I led to believe that it's me that's done something wrong?*

At least, the policeman documented all the information and, in the end, thanked Walter profusely for his contribution, managing to make him feel fairly content as he returned home.

Over the next few days, Walter scanned the newspapers eagerly each day, partly because he now felt to some degree personally involved in the whole business and partly from a purely selfish point of view to establish whether his contribution had been deemed sufficiently important to reach the press. The possibility that the mystery gasser may be a woman did not feature in any article over the first three days, even though the press did their best to keep the story alive by publishing brief articles of little substance in the middle pages, such as that the police were continuing to be vigilant. On the fourth morning, everything changed.

Two days previously, he read, a local teenage girl awoke in the night feeling sick. Fearing that she was about to vomit, she sat up in bed and started to retch, the disturbance wakening her mother and father in an adjacent bedroom. They rushed to attend to her and then suddenly too felt severely nauseated. Within a few minutes, the severe symptoms of all three began to settle so that they were able to discuss what may have caused them all to feel ill about the same time. Fairly quickly, they concluded that the responsibility lay with the hot dogs that the family had bought from a travelling food van the previous evening after they returned from the local baseball match in the nearby park. The mother suggested that she get some water and indigestion tablets for them all. As she rose from sitting on her daughter's bed, her upper body moved well enough but both her legs seemed like deadweights pinned to the floor. The more she tried to lift them, the less they seemed willing to move. She began to breathe heavily and her heart raced and thumped so that she felt her heart might literally jump out of her chest. She collapsed backwards, let her head rest on the pillow next to her daughter and tried to regain control of her feelings. Instinctively, the girl tried to move over to make room for her mother but then realised that she too could move only the upper part of her body; her legs seemed to be stuck to the mattress. She also began to panic or at least, for whatever reason, developed thumping in the chest and rapid breathing.

Despite sharing the other symptoms, her husband found that he was free to move. He ran from the room with ease and went to call for an emergency medical visit. By the time the doctor arrived two hours later, however, all three of them had recovered completely. The nausea, overbreathing and rapid pulse of the women had abated and their legs moved normally. Indeed when the doctor examined them formally, he found no abnormality of power, sensation or reflexes. So far, the symptoms have defied medical explanation, said the article.

He read on. During the same night, a woman was woken from sleep about five o'clock in the morning by the sound of her daughter coughing violently in an adjacent bedroom. When she tried to get out of bed to attend to her daughter, the lady discovered to her horror that she was barely able to move; her legs, in particular, appeared to be paralysed. She dragged herself onto the floor using her arms, managed to pull herself across to the open window and screamed for help. As fortune would have it, a local man, whom she recognised, had just started his shift as a street cleaner and heard her cries. With the aid of some of his work's equipment, he managed to climb onto the roof pitch of the downstairs bay window and hauled himself through the lady's bedroom window. On the mother's instruction, he first went to attend to the daughter who fortunately by then had ceased her coughing attack and was able to accompany him back to her mother. The man kindly called for the doctor. Whilst waiting for him to attend, she reported to the man that she had noticed nothing unusual to explain the incident except for a faint disinfectant-like smell at the open window, an observation confirmed by the daughter. The mother said that she was now inclined to dismiss that observation as irrelevant because she assumed that the smell arose from some chemical that he was using in the street. Significantly, however, the man replied that he was using no chemicals that day. By a few hours later, the mother and daughter had both fully recovered and again, by the time of his attendance, the doctor could find nothing wrong.

Walter read that, having heard of these two incidents on the same night, the police were now stepping up their investigations. They urged anyone who believed that they had suffered similar symptoms, and especially if they thought they had been gassed, to call them at the time as a matter of emergency. They promised to attend the scene immediately with a full police presence in the expectant hope of apprehending the perpetrator before they were able to leave the vicinity. Walter determined that the community had to do everything possible to assist the police and decided to consult with his good friend George on a plan of action.

The following day, a blonde-haired lady in her mid-twenties arrived at the police station.

"I have been a victim of that mystery poisoner, the gasman," Miss Cohen told the officer.

"Tell me about it."

"I had gone to bed as normal and fell asleep ok but I woke up at about two o'clock feeling extremely sick. I thought I was going to throw up but fortunately I didn't. I felt really weak; my arms and legs ached. I didn't really get back to sleep - well, I drifted in and out - but thankfully by the morning I felt a lot better. I wouldn't have thought too much about it - thought it was food poisoning or something like that - but then I read the paper in the morning and realised, oh my God, he's got me too. It's really frightening when you think something like that could happen to you, I can tell you officer. I could have been killed!"

"Did you notice anything - anyone outside or anything like that?"

"No, but at the time I wasn't looking for it. When I think back, I might have noticed a funny smell just like that lady in the paper but I wouldn't have thought much about it at the time. Why would you?"

"Could you move all right? Did your legs work ok?"

"Well, they felt really heavy. I could move them but they didn't feel right. Maybe I was lucky and got only a small dose of the poison."

"Was anyone else with you when you noticed these symptoms?"

"No, I live alone."

The police officer continued with what had by now become a standard series of questions of suspected victims of the mystery gasser and explained that they had now established a procedure whereby everyone who may have been affected is, with their consent, given a standard interview and examination with a doctor who is assisting the police with their enquiries. The main purpose of the assessment, he explained, was to attempt to identify the nature of the poison used in the attacks, which would help to locate its source and the people who may sell the product or regularly deal with it in some capacity. Clearly that evidence would help to find the perpetrator. The lady agreed.

"Well, the examination is entirely normal, Miss Cohen" said Dr. Michaels later, "so whatever caused the problems you experienced seems to have caused no permanent damage."

"Thank goodness! It's terrifying to think that there is someone out there who is intent on hurting people for no reason. Maybe I am the lucky one. Who knows what the others have been left with?"

"Well, actually I do," said the doctor smiling, "and fortunately - so far at least - everyone has been as lucky as you because they have all recovered."

"Sorry, doctor, yes of course you do! I didn't think - but the next one may not be so lucky."

Dr. Michaels decided against continuing this line of unproductive conversation and asked: "Have you had any other significant illnesses in the past or recently?"

"Nothing more that he average person - flu, colds, upset stomachs - that kind of thing."

"Any mental illnesses - anxiety, depression?"

"Well, I had a bout of stress about a year or so ago. But that was when my boyfriend walked out on me after four years together. It came as a big surprise because I wasn't expecting it."

"Any particular reason?"

"He said I had become strange - not sure what he meant - but he picked on a small doll collection I had started and said it was weird for me to get involved in that kind of thing."

"What kind of thing?"

"Honestly, I have no idea. Lots of people collect things and for me it was small dolls but he didn't seem to like it. He said it made him feel creepy."

"Surely that cannot be the only reason?"

"Well, I guess not but that was one of the things he mentioned right off."

"Did you take treatment for the stress?"

"Yes, my doctor put me on some tablets, antidepressants I think."

"Do you remember the name?"

"No, sorry. It was a long word and I don't think I could pronounce it if I wanted to!"

"No, of course. Not to worry. Are you still taking them?"

"I stopped them about six months ago."

"On your doctor's advice?"

"No, I just thought I'd give it a try without them. And I feel fine so I think that was a good thing."

"How did the stress affect you? What symptoms or feelings did you have?"

She was about to answer but paused and looked straight towards the doctor. "Why do you want to know all this?"

"I just need to get as full a picture as possible of the medical details of all the people who have reported some kind of incident related to the mystery prowler. For example, I need to know if any previous condition could have influenced the effect of any poison and the recovery from it."

"Well, ok." She sighed. "For a couple of weeks, I was unable to leave the house. I just sat in a chair feeling lifeless and miserable. I could hardly be bothered to shower - but I did. Then, when I started to go out, I felt really frightened. I didn't like to meet anybody new, even an assistant in a store. Even the people I knew well I found difficult to trust. But it passed eventually."

"With the treatment?"

"Well, I guess so."

Walter settled at the usual table in the usual bar and waited for George. As he sipped on his first beer of the evening, striving to ensure that a respectable amount remained in the bottle by the time his friend arrived, he gazed through the window on to the street. Part of him wanted to see his beloved community just going about its peaceful business undisturbed but another part was hoping to see something that would allow him to rid the town of this menace forever. Absent-mindedly, he put his hand into the inside pocket of his safari jacket and ran his fingers over the barrel of the revolver. Walter was not a violent man by nature but he knew the community had to band together and do whatever was necessary to regain their former way of life, free from danger, free from anxiety. And he knew he would have little difficulty in convincing his long-time friend. But a woman! Could he shoot a woman, however necessary it might seem? In fact, could he shoot anyone? Like many true-blooded Americans, he had kept a gun at home since he was a young man in case of self-defence but prided himself on living in a neighbourhood where he had never had to use it. Until now, perhaps. To date, there had been eight reports of various kinds connected with the prowler and he just knew that this could not be allowed to go on much longer, however hard the police were working on it. *Yes, we all had to pull together.*

George arrived about ten minutes later and picked up the beer that Walter had bought for him and left on the table. After a couple of mouthfuls, he sat down.

"You said you wanted to talk about the mystery gasser. What's on your mind?"

"Something's got to be done, George," said Walter leaning over the table and gazing purposefully into his friend's face. "We've got this lunatic wandering around our community, gassing people at random, or so it seems, and for no particular reason except that he is crazed - or, if you believe me, that she is crazed. They don't threaten; they don't steal; there's no motive that anyone can identify. It's the working of a mad person - and mad people tend to get more mad. No-one has been permanently damaged - or killed - I grant you but that's up to now. You can bet your life that this screwball will get even more disturbed in the head and do something worse and then someone will die for sure. And the longer she is allowed to carry on with no-one able to find out who she is and stop her, the braver - and madder - she is likely to get."

"How sure are you that it is a woman, Walter? Everyone else seems to think it's a man."

"I know, George, but, if you read the reports, no-one except me got a really good look at them. In fact, most people didn't see anyone. They either woke up coughing and unable to move, they smelt something weird or they felt their heart race and couldn't breathe - or all of the above. Just one or two managed to get to the window and saw someone running away but I guess they didn't see much of them. I, on the other hand, saw someone in a skirt, which tells me it was a woman - or a guy who is a bit strange, shall we say, in more ways than one."

"But the police are on the case," said George. "They've stepped up the operations a lot and asked everyone to tell them immediately if they see something odd so that they can attend straight away. Isn't that good enough?"

"It's great, George, but we can help them!"

"OK, Walt, but how? What are you thinking?"

"OK," said Walter drawing his seat closer to the table, "this is how I see it. You, me and anyone else we can find to join us and I am sure we can - Bob, Bill, Joe, Don for starters - take it in turns to walk the streets each night, maybe in twos, making sure that everything is just hunky dory. On the other hand, if we do see something out of hand, we can deal with it - there and then. We wouldn't have to wait for the cops to come which, with the best will in the world, might be some time and frankly too late. We'd catch the madman as I say there and then."

"It seems this guy - or woman if you prefer - is pretty smart at getting away. Neither of us is that young anymore and neither are the other guys you mention. How are we going to outrun them?"

Walter put his hand into his inner pocket and withdrew the revolver just enough for George to glimpse it. "If necessary, we could use one of these." Then he put it back out of sight.

"Now who's the crazy one, Walt?" said George. "More likely than not you'd find yourself on the wrong side of the cops facing a charge of assault or worse!"

"I don't think so, George. For one, we would only use the weapon if we really had to - if there was no other way - and, for two, the cops are desperate to rid this jackass from our midst. They are under a lot of pressure from those in authority to get the community back to normal. They like the idea that we live in this great neighbourhood and that's how they want it to stay - and how they want the rest of the world to perceive it. This gasman - woman - is doing no good for the town's reputation abroad and they want it brought to an end pretty pronto. I think you'd find that, if we did bring this lunatic in, by whatever means necessary, any possible charges against us would be quietly dropped. But, if we're smart, it won't get that far anyway."

"I still think you're crazy. I don't mind doing my bit because I agree that we've got to get rid of this guy - but carrying a gun?" George blew through pursed lips.

"George, you've got a gun, haven't you? So have most of the homes in this town. What for? I'll tell you what for: to protect ourselves against just this sort of threat! Anyway, I've told you: we probably wouldn't have to use it but it's there just in case."

"OK, Walter, I'll join your vigilante band - because that's what it is - and only because I agree that everything should be done that can be done. But you've got to agree not to start any gun-wielding."

"I already have, George, and you know me better than that. Ready to speak to the other guys, then?"

"Yes, ok, I suppose so," said George with another sigh.

George and Walter glanced around the main street before heading off down one of the side roads that led to the network of small streets near where Walter had had his first sighting. It was about an hour after sunset and already the area had assumed its familiar nighttime blackness although a full moon provided more illumination than usual. Light rain collected in small puddles that reflected the moonlight. The two men had brought a flashlight but, to avoid being noticed, had no intention of using it until necessary, hopefully when they succeeded in apprehending their target; the natural light was therefore a bonus.

After two hours, they had completed a tour of the area three times. By now, George was starting to have serious doubts as to whether the whole exercise was worthwhile or, at least, whether he could continue to give up his time in something that seemed ultimately fruitless. After all, he thought, this was the third night in a row that he had spent ambling around the back streets to no avail. However much he enjoyed spending time with his friend, there was a limit and, having to talk in whispers, in the rain and without a beer, reduced its attraction. But just as he was about to share his misgivings with Walter, he heard a scuffling sound coming from further down the street. He turned to alert his friend but Walter had obviously heard it too because he was pointing towards the area from where the noise seemed to come. Straining their eyes to see through the semi-darkness, they saw something moving and then disappear, presumably as it turned into another road. Instinctively, they both began to run; Walter put his hand onto the revolver in his inner pocket but then hastily withdrew it. *No, not a good idea, we decided - at least not yet.*

George reached the corner at the crossroads first but Walter was close behind and they turned into the side road to the right virtually together. Seeing nothing untoward, they stopped, looked around and listened. About fifty yards ahead was another crossroads, bordered by old French-style houses with Juliet balconies on the upper floor. The two men were both very familiar with this part of town and knew that their next steps would be into a virtual maze of narrow nineteenth-century streets where anyone could easily hide. Their prospects of success in their venture were fading fast but to carry on they must.

And then, ten yards down the street to the left, the stillness was broken: a figure jumped out from a doorway to the right and stood in the middle of the road, facing towards them. The body was dark and indistinct but the face seemed to carry its own luminance. The eyes were bright, wide open and staring straight towards them; the mouth was fixed in a half open position, teeth just visible. Although they could not make out details on the body, they could see clearly the overall posture; the head was bent forwards about forty-five degrees and the arms were semi-flexed so that the hands were at the level of the shoulders with the palms facing forwards and the fingers slightly spread. The general demeanour was that of a cat about to pounce.

Now is the time, thought Walter; *now really is the time.* He reached into his inside pocket, wrapped his hand around the handle of the revolver and was about to withdraw it when the inside of his nostrils began to burn; his eyes smarted and watered and he sensed a powerful, chemical-like smell. Soon afterwards, he started coughing violently and his heart pounded. He then began to retch. He tried harder to pull out the gun but the racking movements of his body seemed to hinder every attempt and his vision was by now virtually blinded. Within a few minutes, his legs began to buckle; he staggered and fell to the ground. He tried to stand again but the limbs were becoming increasingly weak and he soon realised it would be impossible. Walter called out to his friend for help but received no answer. He then tried to crawl to the side of the road, hoping to find some support to enable him to stand again, but almost immediately his hand touched on the body of George lying close by and Walter realised that his friend had suffered a similar fate.

"George, are you ok?"

"Yes," said his friend in a faint, croaking voice, "but I can't see and I can hardly move."

"Me neither. What the hell is going on?"

"I guess it's the son of a bitch that we're looking for. We got to get help before it's too late for either of us. Come on - all we can do is shout."

It seemed like an age of mixed shouting, rasping and coughing with both of the men becoming increasingly exhausted but in truth help was by their sides within ten minutes. A middle-aged lady from one of the nearby houses had been alerted by what was an uncommon sound from the streets in that area at night. Using a flashlight, she had seen the men lying in the road outside her window and alerted her husband; the two managed to half drag and half carry them into the house. Once out of the cold, damp outside air, their coughing began to ease and soon they were able to recount their stories. No-one was in much doubt that the phantom gasser had struck again. The lady of the house, who had been avidly following the saga as it developed in the newspapers, felt able to reassure George and Walter that the paralysis would very likely recover within a few hours, something that in their own hearts they knew and had thus far prevented them from undue panic.

As usual, by the time the doctor arrived, the power in their legs was improving although, now primed from earlier cases to make a speedy visit, he was still able to detect residual weakness but no other tell-tale signs. With little more to do, and confident in the likely outcome, the doctor left. The two men did indeed recover physically over the next few hours but they were left with a sense of dismay, dismay that any future actions may be similarly thwarted and that they would be powerless to prevent a recurrence of what had happened this time. Everything had happened so quickly and they did not even see where the poison had come from - or at least did not remember. Next time would they be able to apprehend the perpetrator before he - or she - released their poison? They had to admit that they both harboured serious lingering doubts that they would, doubts that would have been anathema to them when they first planned their vigilante missions. And they were also left with the image of the face, one that they knew would never be erased from their memory: the shining face, burning eyes, leering and predatory mouth. What creature was this? Was it truly human? What powers did it have; what powers could it yet unleash?

For the rest of that day, Walter and George did nothing but the next day they met, partly to discuss their next plan of action but partly, with only subconscious realisation, to provide spiritual support to each other and allow them to resume some sense of normality.

"All things considered, you look ok," said George, "if maybe a bit pale. But I guess, like me, you didn't sleep too well last night."

"No," said Walter, "but I have to say better than I expected - and no bad dreams, thank the Lord!"

As they knew, a couple of lunch-time beers can work wonders for relaxation and focus and the two took advantage of the fact. Towards the end of the second, their conversation began to open up.

"So now what?" asked George.

"I've been thinking about it," said Walter, "and I've got a couple of ideas. First, we've got to tell the police - obviously, because they need as much evidence as they can get."

"I guess the doctor will have passed on his report," said George. "They all seem now to have set up a pretty good organisation - the police, doctors and so on - so the cops probably know. In fact, if we were at home, we'd probably have them knocking on the door by now."

"Sure," said Walter, "but we still have to give them the details. The second thing is that we have to share our experience and thoughts with the other folk in our community and see if we can work out together what this beast is about and what they might do next. We've got to catch it somehow. I suggest we call a meeting."

"Good idea. And maybe ask if the cops and the doctor would come too. They might be happy to share their thoughts with us all to get as much cooperation as possible. And at least they could use the meeting to blunt any mounting community panic. After all, the longer this goes on, the more desperate people become."

"That's good, George! I'll contact the police and put it to them just like you say. Meanwhile let's get on and book the hall and put up some notices around the town. If you do the hall, I'll organise the notices."

Within forty-eight hours, all the groundwork was done. The town hall was booked for a week hence; the police captain had agreed to come to the meeting with the doctor assigned to the cases; Walter had persuaded a local printer to rush out some notices free of charge; and he and George had pinned them at strategic points in the neighbourhood to attract maximal attention. By three days later, about one hundred people had contacted Walter, as requested on the notices, to confirm that they would be attending.

At Walter's request, the police captain conducted the meeting from the stage at the front, his audience huddled together on removable chairs in a room that was barely large enough to accommodate the number present. Inevitably, the course of the meeting was interrupted from time to time by the noise of someone scraping the chair across the floor as they struggled to achieve a more comfortable position but overall it was manageable.

The police captain began by explaining the situation to date. After the first five minutes, during which Walter felt that he recounted what every single person in the room already knew - otherwise they would not have been there - he started on the detail. Over the previous five weeks, there had been a total of sixteen people reporting unexplained attacks on one or more members of the household. In all episodes, except for the attack on the men in the street and one less clear attack reported by a woman in her twenties, at least one of the people affected in each attack was a teenage girl. Often, someone had been awoken by the noise of a prowler outside their home; in most of the attacks, about the same time, someone in the household had become acutely ill with coughing, retching, rapid heart rate and breathlessness; most of these victims had been subsequently temporarily paralysed. In eight cases, someone in the house, the victim or another person, had detected an unusual smell, variously described as like ammonia, cleaning fluid or even flowers. In addition, four people had reported being woken by a strange smell but had suffered no symptoms. Despite most of the people, or a relative, being able to get to the window, only six reported seeing anybody acting strangely, in all cases someone running away from the house. Five of these observers believed that person to be male, the other female. The captain then made reference to the sighting by Walter that the individual was probably female although on that occasion none of the other features - the smell, choking, paralysis and so on - were present so the police could not be sure that this sighting was connected to the others, specifically that the individual observed was the same. Finally, he referred to the experience of the two men in the street; here the features of the attack were similar to others but, beyond a terrifying appearance, few details of the perpetrator were available.

Walter could not help feeling that the evidence of George and him was being a little glossed over but, apart from a knowing glance to his friend, he let it pass.

The captain then invited Doctor Patterson to address the audience before returning to discuss what the police operation was about and how members of the community could assist their endeavours. The doctor explained that, to say the least, the situation was unusual. To a layman, it may seem obvious that somebody was simply going about the neighbourhood gassing people but, when examined critically from a medical perspective, not everything was easily accounted for. First, although all the cases seemed at first glance to be the same, there were, in fact, quite a few differences among them, which would be unusual, at least if the same poison was being used on every occasion. Secondly, said the doctor, the symptoms that were reported by the victims were not entirely typical of those produced by any of the poisons that were readily available to a member of the general public. Taken in isolation, some of the effects were known to result from the common poisons but, when all symptoms were taken together, the picture that emerged was very unusual. So, he concluded, either the perpetrator was using some rare type of poison or the effects on the victims were created by some other mechanism.

"Such as what?" said a man near the front.

"Well, at this stage, I don't know," replied the doctor, "but all possibilities need to be borne in mind. Maybe the differences amongst the cases is because the cause is not always the same. I can assure you that the medical team is still working hard to provide an explanation and, as far as we are able, we are in touch with some of the experts in this type of illness throughout the rest of the country."

At the end of the meeting, Walter and George ambled together along the main street before each going their separate ways home.

"Can't say that that achieved much!" said Walter.

"Well, certainly not what we had hoped, I guess. I for one feel more confused now than I was before we went in there," said his friend.

"Me too."

"It seemed to me that the police were saying that they are going to carry on with their in-depth enquiries, that they will respond immediately to any call for help and that the public should be diligent in observing what is going on around them and keep out of danger!" continued George.

"I guess that's all true," replied Walter, "and, to be fair, what else can they do? They are being pretty attentive."

"And what about that doctor?" said George. "Far from giving us a decent medical account, he said in effect that there wasn't one, that it all remains unexplained - even though to a simple guy like me, and possibly the rest of the world, it seems pretty darned obvious that someone is going around gassing people. I think sometimes these experts think too much!"

"Just supposing he's right," said Walter, "and it cannot all be explained by poisoning, well simple poisoning shall we say, what else could it be?"

"If you ask me," said George, after a minute or two's thought, "let me tell you this: I was brought up to believe that, if something goes badly wrong and you cannot find out how or why it happened, if there is no good explanation, if no person seems to be to blame and it's against all the laws of nature, then it's probably evil at work."

"Like what sort of evil?"

"Evil forces."

"Evil forces? Do you mean nasty people?"

"They can be acted out through people but there are forces behind those people that you cannot detect."

"Oh, come on, George," said Walter, "do you really believe all that? Yes, I was brought up to believe in the world of spirits as well but I have since realised that the earth goes round the sun and not the other way round!"

"Don't try and be funny, Walt. This is not the time." Then, after a pause: "Anyway, do you really not think that some things are brought about by evil. Because I do."

"Well, maybe," said Walter, "but something like this? Anyway, when something does happen that you might describe as evil, you usually still find that there's some person behind it."

"They are just the agent. The real force is somewhere else."

"So, supposing you are right, we still have to find this agent, as you call it. We are back to square one."

"Except that the person we are looking for is likely to be the kind of person who has connections with the spiritual world, the world of evil. We have to look for that type of person."

"Are you saying connections with the Devil? You may as well come out and say it, if that's what you think! Or are you worried that I will think you even more crazy than I do now?!"

"Well, I don't mean some creature with horns and a tail, if that's what you are suggesting. Even we Devil-believers have become a bit more sophisticated over the years! No, Walt, if you do believe even a bit that there are forces of evil that work

60

outside the laws of nature, then we need to find the agent who is acting them out. Agreed or not?"

Walter paused for a few minutes, then took a deep breath. "The logical part of me wants to say that you are talking garbage but I admit there is another bit of me that doesn't want to rule anything out. We've certainly got to sort this out, whatever it takes to do it."

"I believe it was you who suggested to me that we should be looking for someone who is new to the area because, unless one of our long-term residents has suddenly gone crazy, that is the only decent explanation of why things have changed here. And, to my eye, old Dorothy Crowe down at the grocery store is no more crazy than she has ever been!"

"Guess not!" said Walter with a laugh.

Wandering further down the street, they came to a crossroads where they would normally turn right. Still deep in conversation, and on a route that was fairly automatic for them, they paid little attention to what was going on around them so perhaps it was not too surprising that they almost knocked over the elderly lady coming around the corner towards them.

"Alice, I am so sorry!" said Walter as he reached out to prevent her falling. "We were so engrossed in what we were talking about that we didn't seem to notice anything else - including you, I am very sorry to say!"

"It's ok, Walt. No harm done. It must have been something pretty important that occupied you though, I guess," she said with a laugh.

"Well, we were just talking about the mystery gasser, which we seem to be doing most of the time these days."

"Isn't everybody?" said Alice. "What's your latest take on it?"

"Ah, well! George here thinks it's all the work of the Devil and that somebody in this community of ours is acting as his agent!"

He started to laugh nervously but was stopped by her reply: "I must say I agree with him, Walt. Not only that but I can have a pretty good guess who it is." She stared meaningfully into his eyes.

"And?" said Walter.

"That woman on Tuscola Avenue. You know her - thin, skimpy brown hair, glasses - came to live here about a year ago but you don't see her very much. She keeps herself to herself, well her and her cat. Why doesn't she mix with the rest of us? Mark my words, Walter, that woman is up to no good!"

"Oh, come on, Alice," said Walter, "can you really say that? What evidence do you have? Maybe she is just shy."

"The evidence, Walter, is that nothing has gone right since she came here. Isn't that enough? We used to live in a peaceful community where things happened like clockwork, as night follows day. But since she came, everything has gone wrong, starting with that poor child of the Wilsons, who died suddenly for no obvious reason. Then there was the train crash with all those girls on board - and now this!"

"Coincidence? Just possibly - maybe?" said Walter with heavy sarcasm.

"You may jeer, Walter, but you won't be jeering when things start to get even more horrible and you find out - maybe just a bit too late - that I was right after all!" During the pause when Walter was thinking of something apposite to say, she took the opportunity to press home her point: "And I am not the only one who thinks this, either. Just ask around - Betty Harris, Virginia Adams, Anna O'Connell for starters - and you'll find that they - and a whole lot more besides - realise something that apparently you do not!"

The force of her statement had stunned Walter and unusually he was stuck for words. Eventually, as she continued to stare at him, all he could think of to say was, "Well, maybe." She said no more, shook her head and walked briskly on her way.

Walter turned to George who had remained silent throughout the exchange. "I guess you've found one person to support your crazy ideas."

"More than one, by the sound of it," said George quietly and looking towards the ground.

"OK, George, let's try and be rational. Let's look at the evidence for this story. What do you know about this woman?"

"Well, not a lot," said George, looking up. "I know who Alice was talking about and I know that she's called Annie Murphy. But not much else because, as Alice said, she has kept herself to herself in that small house on Tuscola Avenue since she came here about a year ago."

"I know that much, George; I know that much. So how does that make her a criminal?"

"In itself, obviously it doesn't," said George, becoming more animated. "it's all just a bit odd. Why would someone want to behave like that? And, when something goes wrong that you can't explain, you have to look for unusual things - or an unusual person, as I've said. We know most of the folks around her very well so we can rule them out as mischief-makers.

Then the finger of blame can only be pointed at someone you don't know well and therefore cannot rule out, even more so if they behave in a weird way and are new to the community."

"I don't think that kind of evidence would stand up in a court of law!" said Walter.

"Well, it's pretty much what you said yourself, Walt."

"I agree that we have to start with that kind of person - a stranger, in particular - but that's where we start. You then have to see if there is any evidence to implicate them. You cannot string them up on the basis of the kind of evidence that you were talking about - that they seem to be a bit odd."

"OK, let's see what we can find out," said George. "Agreed?"

"Agreed!"

Betty Harris and Virginia Adams were taking coffee together, as they did most weeks on Tuesday and Friday mornings. They were both brought up in New Amboise, had known each other since childhood and had become close friends since moving into Tuscola Avenue about the same time four years earlier. Indeed, Betty had not completely emptied all the packing cases and put away her household belongings into their new home by the time that Virginia's removal truck arrived two doors down. Both being new to the street and with the common aim of setting up a new home, it seemed natural that they should help each other to settle in as quickly as they could, particularly since the layout of the two houses was virtually identical. Not only did they provide mutual assistance with the practical matters, but they also gave each other advice on how the homes would be most tastefully arranged and on the most efficient use of the cupboards and other storage spaces and offered emotional support to each other for the commoner stresses associated with moving house. Thus they bonded during those early weeks and their friendship continued to develop as they realised that they shared general thoughts on the world, senses of value and morality and even a difficult-to-define way of thinking. Without ever having to force the situation, they seemed to agree on most matters and certainly never argued.

When Annie Murphy moved into the house between the two of theirs three years later, their memories of the benefits they had gained from their mutual assistance at the time of their own removals had not completely faded and they were keen to welcome a new addition to their close relationship. So, as the slight, brown-haired lady with glasses walked hesitatingly from the removal truck to her new front door, Betty and Virginia appeared simultaneously from their houses to greet her literally with open arms. But sadly their good intentions were not well received; with barely a word, the newcomer diverted her gaze and, after a simple "Good morning, thank you", entered her new home and closed the door, reappearing only when she was sure that her neighbours had retreated back into their own houses.

On this particular coffee morning, almost exactly twelve months later, Betty and Virginia were rehearsing their conversations from earlier meetings, as they usually did, including their conclusions that the town square was not swept often enough, that prices at the local store were excessive and the owner must be making unreasonable profits and that one day some child will suffer a mishap if parents continued to allow them to wander at will around the streets without supervision. They agreed that they were both fortunate that neither had had children of their own and indeed were better off alone without a man in tow.

Inevitably, the conversation moved to the more serious subject of the mystery gasser, on which, over recent weeks, each of the two women had reinforced the views of the other in a series of speculative interchanges that over time had developed into impressions of virtual certainties in their minds. And those subjective certainties included their neighbour, Annie Murphy. It was particularly unfortunate that Annie lived in the house directly between those of the other two women because she was thereby the focus of attention from either side, metaphorically trapped in a vice of judgement.

"Not much moving on the gasser front, is there?" said Virginia, returning from the kitchen holding cups replenished with more coffee.

"Certainly isn't! We keep hearing that the police are doing all they can and are working their butts off to catch her but then they do nothing."

"Because they are looking in the wrong place! As we know well but nobody listens to us, I guess because we are just two sad women, in their eyes at any rate. You never know - maybe one day they will."

"Well, we've told them, haven't we but what do we get in response? That they cannot do anything without evidence. I ask you: how much evidence do they need?"

"Couldn't agree more, Betty, as you know. I ask you - did you see her go out the other evening, just as night was approaching? Where was she going, what was she up to, alone when it's nearly dark? Did she meet anyone? Well, nobody that I have spoken to, I can tell you."

"Or me."

"And it's not the first time," continued Betty. "I've taken to sitting at the window come the evening and I can tell you she goes out pretty often on her own as it's getting dark."

"I know," said Virginia. "I've seen it too."

"Some people have said that she likes to go for a walk."

"A walk!" said Virginia with an exaggerated laugh. "In the dark?!"

"You don't need to convince me, Virginia, but that's what they say."

"You can't stop people talking bullshit, I guess. Did you hear those noises again last night?"

"Sure did. Horrible screeching - came from her bedroom, I think."

"Definitely, just as before. Don't tell me - it's her playing with her cat!"

"That's what some folk say, as you know."

"Bullshit again! I'll tell you what she's up to. Why is it always the bedroom? Is that the only place she plays with her cat? No, that woman is having sex with the Devil!"

"That's what witches do, my friend. That's what they do," said Betty in a tone of resignation.

"I'll tell you, Betty, people will realise in the end. And then maybe somebody, somewhere will finally rid us of this evil woman. We can't get rid of the Devil but we can sure get rid of his agents here on earth!"

"Well, I think they are realising, Virginia, slowly I grant you. But speaking around, I find that more and more people are coming to learn the truth. I was talking to a group of women waiting at the station the other day - Pat Howard, Lilian Gray and Rose Petersen amongst them - and rest assured that they are thinking the same way as we are. They've seen her come and go in her furtive little ways and are in not much doubt that she is up to no good. Put two and two together and what do you get?"

"You get to know who the gasser is, that's what you get!"

The two women's conversation was becoming increasingly agitated and, after a while, even they had to stop for a rest. By now breathing heavily, wide-eyed and flushed about the face, they both settled into silence and stared at the floor. A few minutes later, now calmer, Virginia lifted her head and looked at her friend.

"Something's got to be done, Betty; that's for sure."

"I agree."

The local gossip had not escaped the attention of Annie Murphy. Indeed, it had increased to such a level over the course of a few weeks that it would have been difficult for anyone to ignore. Annie became acutely aware of the looks and whispers wherever and whenever she went anywhere near other people. It was true that generally she did not willingly mix with others but she had to go about the routine business of life just like anybody else. Whilst she deliberately chose the times that the streets were less populated, such as when the shops first opened in the morning or when most of the rest of the community was engaged in traditional one o'clock lunches, she could not avoid everybody. Previously, those she encountered had ignored her as she ignored them, having become accustomed to her isolationism since the early days of her arrival in the town when they had tried, unsuccessfully, to befriend her. But now the situation had changed. When she entered a shop, those already present moved closer into a group, lowered their voices and gave sideways glances towards her. Sometimes they stared openly at her, at best meaningfully and at worst malevolently. Even the shopkeepers had changed. Again previously used to not engaging in conversation, they had now taken on an air of reluctance to serve her at all. Her bought items were pushed or even thrown brusquely towards her; eye contact was avoided; and they stood back seemingly as far as they could as if to minimise contracting some serious infectious disease.

But if this change of heart amongst her neighbours bothered her, she did not show it. She continued, as before, to carry out her activities with the greatest efficiency and the least possible display of emotion. The consequent difficulty in determining what she was thinking unfortunately increased the suspicions of those around her, resulting in an increasingly upward spiral of suspicion and distrust. Eventually, even though Annie's behaviour had not altered, her position in the community changed from that of a strange recluse to one of dangerous pariah. But Annie carried on; even when the mark appeared on the wall of the house, she seemed, outwardly at least, unconcerned.

Walter was walking home from his game of eight-ball pool in the community hall on Western Avenue. The game had finished earlier than usual because some of the men had to go on to an anniversary celebration and it was still light. A pleasant evening, Walter decided to take a detour from the direct route back to his house and, at first, simply wandered aimlessly among the streets, thinking little and enjoying the atmosphere created by the cardinals' singing from the tops of the trees. But, as he reached the sign for Tuscola Avenue, his mental attitude focussed. *Annie Murphy! Let's see what we can find out, I think we said. OK, here we go!* After allowing a brief smile to himself, Walter turned left into the avenue. One part of him considered this to be a fruitless exercise, apart from continuing a pleasant walk in the evening air, because, after all, he knew this part of town very well and what was he likely to discover that he did not already know? But another part felt a degree of sympathy with George's opinions and he had promised to go along with his friend in finding out whether there was any substance in his suspicions. By the time Virginia Adams's house came into distant view, the light was beginning to fade but Walter could still see sufficiently clearly to detect anything untoward. The bedroom light in the house next door was on whilst the downstairs was unlit but there were no shadows or other signs of movement to suggest what Annie might be doing.

Walter reached the front of Annie's house and looked upwards for signs of activity. He scanned the bedroom window but all he could see was the unfettered light streaming through the uncurtained window. As he shifted his gaze to the right, his attention was caught abruptly by something on the side wall of the house, near to the front and about six feet from the ground. *What the hell is that? That wasn't there before, I'm sure,* he thought. He walked closer to the building and studied what seemed to be an elaborate piece of graffiti scratched or carved into the fabric of the building. On further inspection, Walter made out the details of the inscription, which consisted of a series of interlocking rings, formed into the shape of a circle, in the middle of which were a series of straight lines at angles. *That looks like the letter V, mixed with the letter M,* he decided. *What the hell is going on? I can't imagine someone like Annie Murphy has chosen to have that put there for decoration. And what does VM mean? AM for Annie Murphy, maybe, but VM?*

He examined the remainder of the side wall and the rest of the exterior but found nothing more. He turned to set off home but, before he had taken a few steps, he heard a faint but definite high-pitched noise seemingly stemming from the upstairs room. Turning back to look, he could now see ill-defined shadows moving across what was previously a blank canvas of light from the bedroom window. He concentrated to listen as the noise continued, possibly for three or four minutes before abating. The noise was not quite like anything he had heard before and he could not identify it precisely. *A cat? She does have a cat. But it doesn't sound a very happy cat, if that's what it is.* Walter waited for five more minutes or so but neither the noise nor the movements returned and he set off home. *Well, that's something to talk about with George, at any rate.*

As he turned left off Tuscola Avenue back on to the main street home, he passed a church on his left, which he had done many times before without thinking. On this occasion, however, for some reason his eyes settled on the main sign outside the entrance on to the street. *The Church of the Holy Virgin Mary, CHVM. VM? There it is again! A coincidence, surely.* Walter walked on.

Unusually, Walter did not sleep well that night. He went to bed with uncommon fatigue on arriving home and fell asleep fairly quickly but, around three a.m., he awoke with a start from a dream, the kind of which he had never experienced before. Also, unlike many dreams, he was able to recall all the details after wakening. Walter had been in a dark pit with glimmers of light filtering from above down a long chimney-like cavern just sufficient for him to discern the things that were around him. At first, all he could see were dark, damp, walls of unhewn rock but, as he became more accustomed to the low light, he detected small insects crawling among the gaps between the stones. But these did not resemble any insects that he knew. Their legs were short and stubby, their bodies fat, almost circular, and their heads were disproportionately large. The mouths were wide and slightly upturned at the edges; however much Walter tried to dismiss the idea, he could not avoid the impression that they were smiling. Some of them were burying their heads into gaps in the stone to feed from material that seemed to lie underneath the most superficial layer of rock. Walter gazed into one of the wider cracks where six or seven insects were feeding together; the source of their food bore a disturbing resemblance to human flesh. He began to move to look closer but suddenly the cavern was filled with a deep purple light and, on the wall directly opposite him, appeared a motionless face in black and white. *Annie Murphy!*

Walter recoiled in horror, collapsed backwards and involuntarily closed his eyes. But not for long before the voice forced him to open them again and sit bolt upright - a deep, snarling, obviously threatening tone. *Carry on, Walter, and you will be in this place for ever! Leave her alone; leave her alone; leave her alone!* Walter stared at the face on the opposite wall but it was obvious that the voice did not come from that image, which remained immobile; it was equally obvious that the voice was too deep, too almost non-human, to be that of Annie Murphy. And then he woke.

Walter sat on the edge of the bed with his face in his hands, trembling. His body felt ice-cold; his lips were numb and he could feel the force of his rapid heartbeat down the sides of his neck and over the back of his head. He lifted his head, wiped the sweat from his brow and looked towards his bedroom window, fully expecting the content of his dream to be somehow enacted out there, in real life. But all he saw was darkness. He turned on his bedside light, looked around the room and slowly relished in the normality and familiarity of what he saw: the wicker chair in the corner, the carpet buckled against the wardrobe, fragments of mud just inside the door, the picture of the old lady in a hat on the wall opposite his bed. He took a deep breath and looked again. *Home, yes home. Where did I buy that picture? It was a dream, Walter, a dream. That mud needs cleaning up. A dream, just a dream.* He took another deep breath, stood and walked to the window. Just darkness. *It was a dream, Walter, just a dream.*

Walter spent the next morning sitting in his favourite chair in his living room, alternately drowsing and staring abstractly towards the opposite wall in thought. He knew in his heart that he was just tired, having slept fitfully after his dream, but he could not help thinking, thinking about an experience he had never had before and what it might mean, if anything. Yes, it was a dream but its content did create new ideas, new thoughts on what was going on around him. Could there be any truth in this Devil business and was it just possible that somehow Annie

Murphy was connected with it, as George seemed to believe? *But it was a dream, wasn't it?*

By the end of the morning, Walter felt that he had, in intermittent bouts, caught up on his sleep and that normality, whatever that meant, was returning. He decided to get some air, put on his coat and opened his front door. *No, Walt, you are not going back to Tuscola Avenue.* He turned left. Five or six minutes later, he was settled in the diner on the corner of two streets, drinking coffee and looking abstractedly through the window down one of the streets. Real normality had returned. He took out the notebook and pencil from his inside pocket and began to sketch out some ideas.

"Hello, Walt!" came a voice from behind his shoulder. "How are you?"

Walter pushed his notebook to one side, away from sight, and turned around. "Oh, hello, Virginia. Good to see you. I'm fine; how are you?"

"Good!"

"Are you alone?" said Walter. And then standing up and gesturing, "Please, sit down - have some coffee. Do join me."

"Thanks, Walt! Why not?" And she sat at one of the spare seats at the table.

"So what's new?" she said, as Walter brought over her coffee from the counter.

"Well, quite a lot as it turns out." Walter decided not to give Virginia a full account of what he had experienced because, still harbouring considerable scepticism, he did not want to fuel the beliefs about evil influences in the community that he knew she, and an increasing number of others, held deeply. But Virginia was the type of person who knew most of what was going on around her, and indeed made it her business to do so. So he decided to find out what, if anything, she knew about the new mural on Annie Murphy's wall.

"Have you seen that new thing that's appeared on the outside of Annie Murphy's house, an inscription you might call it?"

"Which one?"

"It's on the side wall, like a design, with circles and lines?"

"As a matter of fact, I have" said Virginia. Thought so, said Walter to himself.

"And what do you make of it? Any idea could have put it there and why?"

"No idea. But it looks like a sort of magic symbol."

"Magic symbol?" said Walter. "What kind of magic symbol? And for what?"

"Funnily enough," she replied, "I was reading a book the other day about witches and other supernatural things. It turns out that people used to draw or carve designs on the houses where the witches lived in order to send them away - to stop them doing any more harm. I guess that's what this might be. Somebody has put the design there to get rid of Annie Murphy."

Somebody, thought Walter. *And I wonder who that might be.* "You certainly seem to know a lot about it, Virginia. What do you make of the letters, VM then?"

"Don't know for sure. Maybe it's the Virgin Mary." *Maybe indeed.*

"And tell me - did your reading indicate that these symbols or designs actually worked?" He tried to limit the tone of scepticism in his voice.

"Seems so," she said. "Sure seems so."

"What happens if the person living in the house is not a witch after all and people have made a mistake? Do the symbols send them away too? Or does it only work with witches?"

"Oh, I think the innocent people have nothing to fear because they are not perpetrators of evil. If there is no evil to dispel, then the symbols cannot work because they are designed specifically to get rid of evil. So those who are not agents of evil are not affected."

"Well, that all sounds very clear cut and straightforward," said Walter, this time not quite managing to disguise his scepticism. "I guess it could even be used as some kind of diagnostic test - if the images get rid of the person, ergo they are a witch; if not, they are innocent!"

"You may jeer," said Virginia, "but I am only telling you what I have read. You can believe it or not."

"And you do?"

"Well, since you ask, I do, yes." *Thought so again.*

"Well, let's see if it works," said Walter, clearly closing the topic.

When later the two had said their goodbyes, Walter decided that he would go and see George, hopefully for a dose of what seems to pass for normality in those days. But first he went for a walk in the fresh air. Although it was a bright afternoon, there was a cool breeze, which he relished as it seemed to settle his mind. There was no doubt that Walter was troubled because, to him, none of the likely future outcomes of the events that had taken over his beloved community were to be welcomed and what he really hoped and prayed for was a return to life as it was. Maybe the mystery gasser would be caught and that would be an end to it but progress in that direction seemed to be absent, however hard the police seemed to be trying. And only four days earlier, another two people had been attacked in their homes by someone, something, outside - the same pattern: a strange smell, coughing, choking and paralysis. Yes, as with others before, they had recovered but this time the paralysis had gone on for longer. Would, one day, the people not recover at all, be permanently paralysed or even die? And what about the mounting hysteria centring around Annie Murphy? Would she become the innocent victim of a vigilante attack? And supposing, just supposing, she were a witch, what other misfortune could she bestow upon the town? Stupid as it seemed to anyone with a rational way of thinking, maybe the best outcome would be if that ridiculous design put on the outside of her house really did work and sent her away. And then there was the dream - although that was just a dream, wasn't it?

"Is it too early for a beer?" said Walter, as George opened his front door.

"Never too early for a beer. I'll get my coat."

They settled into their favourite bar and Walter recounted his experiences of the previous twenty-four hours. He and George had known each other long enough, and had formed a close friendship, that he knew that whatever he told George would be taken seriously, even though they often disagreed on principles. Nevertheless, so stunning had Walter found the events he had to relate that he proceeded cautiously at first until he was sure that his friend was truly engaging. But he need not worry for George displayed an uncommon interest and indeed reacted with more than his usual display of emotion, which varied from surprise to grave concern. Then, as Walter's story progressed and, comforted by his friend's reaction, he opened up more, George became increasingly ponderous and said little.

"So what do you make of it all?" said Walter when he had finished.

George took a deep breath, looked across to the far side of the bar, pressed his lips together and paused. After a minute or two, he spoke:

"I'm inclined to think that your dream was just that - a dream - but it does make you think. As for the rest, well maybe this Annie Murphy is the agent of the Devil here in New Amboise. Those goings-on that you heard in the bedroom sound really weird."

"But it could have been her cat," said Walter.

"Sure, sure. But also maybe not. What is more obvious is that somebody has taken it upon themselves to carve something into her house wall that they believe is going to rid us all of Annie Murphy and, with her, the menace that is going on around us. And, like you, I wouldn't be surprised if that somebody were Virginia Adams or one of her partners-in-crime - and I say partners-in-crime because that's what it is, carving things on other people's houses. Sure, we want to do what we have to do but, like I told you when you had the gun, we've got to keep things proportionate and not let things get out of hand. My worry is that whoever has put that symbol on Annie Murphy's house would not necessarily stop there. You know that I'm drawn to think that there could well be some evil influence here but we've gone past the days of the lynch mob - or, at least, I hope we have."

"Very wise, as usual, George."

"I really think that we could be replacing one disaster in our neighbourhood with another, if Virginia and her crew - if that's who it is - work themselves up into a frenzy and do something stupid. The police wouldn't look too kindly on it; they would end up in serious trouble - gaol or worse; it would be no good for our community spirit; and who knows what other repercussions there might be?"

"Repercussions? Like what?"

"Well, if there are supernatural forces, what are they going to unleash next, if we 'take out', shall we say, one of their number?"

"Maybe that's going a bit far, George - that last bit, I mean."

"Well, maybe but, as always, maybe not."

The two men, and most of the others in the town, had been put off continuing with their nightly vigils of the region after the attack, presumably from the gasser, that had laid them low earlier on. But, after a while, despite their experience they and a few other men had decided to resume when it became clear that the gasser's malevolent activities were continuing.

A key motivation in this decision was the assault on the Robinson twins. The two five-year-old girls had been put to bed by their mother as usual around seven o'clock and she had settled down in a chair in the family living room to read a book. Mrs. Robinson had managed to get the girls into kindergarten just a couple of months before and had started a part-time job in the local hardware store with hours that fitted well with the children's schooling. But it had been some time since she worked formally and she was still getting used to the fatigue that comes initially with any new venture, especially since there was quite a physical element to the job, stocking the shelves with various items of ironwork and lifting them out for customers.   Thus she relished the brief period of relaxation between getting the children to bed and preparing dinner in time for her husband's arrival home an hour or so later.

The neighbours opposite had themselves become accustomed to Mrs. Robinson's new habits, seeing the light go out in the children's bedroom followed soon after by illumination of the lamp in the living room that overlooked the street and the settling down of the mother in the chair next to the window. They would often smile in empathy at the obvious expression of relief displayed in their neighbour's bodily posture as she sank into a position of comfort and lifted her book from the adjacent table. On this day, the lady in the house opposite, Peggy Collins, had again witnessed this sequence of events as she passed by her own window and could not resist a brief frisson of pleasure shared with the close-knit family that seemed to have settled into a routine of mutual happiness. The two girls were identical, not only in being blessed with the same good looks but also intelligence, charm, sweetness and kind nature that belied their very young age.   It was a pleasure to have the family as neighbours.

Mrs. Collins was thereafter occupied in setting the table for the family dinner and did not notice that Mrs. Robinson had risen from her chair much earlier than usual. Not, that is, until she heard the screams coming from the street. Peggy ran to the window and stared into the impending darkness; maybe it was the acute sense of drama that had overtaken her but the street seemed much gloomier than usual for that time of day. But the figure of her neighbour was unmistakeable. Barefooted, Lucille Robinson was running purposelessly back and forth along the street, her hair gripped by her hands over both sides of her head, eyes wide, mouth open and screaming constantly. At one point, she stumbled and fell hard onto her right elbow but undeterred she stood rapidly and continued her mindless motion. Three or four of the doors leading directly on to the street opened virtually simultaneously and within seconds Lucille was in the arms of several men and women doing their best to provide comfort for an as yet unknown tragedy. And so it was: the forces of evil had taken their youngest victims so far. During the twelve hours that followed, their mother would never know whether the total paralysis of her darling children would ever recover and the emotional trauma that was inflicted upon her and those who shared in her grief was profound. But, as usual - as usual so far, said everyone afterwards - they did recover but the effects on the community did not. The sense of betrayal by a person or thing still unidentified was magnified on this occasion by his, her or its choice of two icons of innocence, who so much more than any victim so far had done nothing in their short life to deserve what they received.

And so Walter and George were back pacing the narrow back streets of New Amboise in semi-darkness, sometimes meeting and exchanging a few words with their fellow members of the neighbourhood watch but often now walking together is silence, having previously exhausted topics of conversation that seemed appropriate to the circumstances. Against their more rational judgement, but in reality without much conscious deliberation, they tended to focus their attention around Annie Murphy's house but experienced nothing alarming. They would stop and study the icon on the side of the house but it did not change and no new designs appeared. They stopped and listened but heard no recurrence of the strange noises that Walter had experienced. On two or three occasions, they had watched from a distance and seen Annie Murphy leave the house after dark but, despite all attempts to follow her rapidly albeit surreptitiously, they had lost her before they could witness her in any malevolent act. On one of those occasions, there had followed another gassing event about an hour later but the two men were several streets away at the time; neither had any of the other men been in the area. It seemed as if the perpetrator they sought was well aware, not only of their general presence on the streets, but also the specific location of the men at any one time. Everyone in the neighbourhood watch admitted to mounting frustration, particularly at the notion that they might be being outwitted, but they determined to continue. They also consoled themselves with the thought that, despite lack of success in their primary aim, their activities were not without value for they had succeeded in thwarting an attempted theft of a bicycle from one of the gardens and in aborting the unwanted attentions of one of the local young men on one of the prettier waitresses as she returned home from work.

The local newspapers continued to report each new gassing event as it occurred but otherwise had gone generally quiet in respect of the investigation, perhaps not surprisingly because nothing new transpired as the weeks went by. One morning, however, many of the residents were surprised by a story considered by the editors to be of sufficient importance to feature on the front page. Most people who read it had a reaction of one kind or another. George felt even more frustrated; Walter was pensive; and Virginia was outraged. The story concerned the latest report to the police from the principal doctor involved with the medical aspects of the cases. He provided up-to-date details of the toxicology investigations, including tests on the blood samples of the victims not only for common poisons that might be easily available in that part of the country but also some rarer ones from more distant parts of the USA and even from abroad. Without exception, these tests were negative. The report also provided a new analysis of the symptoms experienced by the victims, including an independent assessment by an expert in medical conditions caused by poisoning from Boston, which showed that the pattern of illness varied greatly amongst the victims. There were certainly many similar general features, such as the coughing, watering eyes and paralysis, but also many that varied, including the time course of onset, development and recovery, the presence or absence of a smell, the nature of that smell, sometimes sweet, sometimes acrid, and other symptoms such as itching and dizziness. The conclusion was that the symptoms experienced by the victims could not be attributed with confidence to poisoning, at least in every case, and it was incumbent upon an unbiased, scientific investigator to consider other possibilities.

Next in the story came the part that really aroused its readers. The investigating panel drew attention to other illnesses that over the centuries had afflicted a large number of people within a close community and for which no rational medical explanation could be found. On more than one of these occasions, subsequent commentators had raised the possibility that the symptoms were spread from one person to another not through any physical mechanism but via a primary psychological process. It may have been, it was suggested, that one or two people became ill from some simple, natural physical process but others then imagined that they had contracted the same condition and displayed the symptoms as a subconscious reaction to that belief. This sort of psychological reaction would be more likely to develop when there was a delay in the diagnosis of the original cases who had a true physical disease because the elements of fear and uncertainty as to who else may develop the condition would be more profound. Eventually, a kind of mass paranoia occurs and many people imagine they have become ill. Because the exact symptoms depend upon the precise psychological reaction of an individual, the condition would vary much more than in illnesses caused by a physical agent.

"What the hell does that mean?" said Betty, as she read the newspaper handed to her by Virginia.

"It means," said Virginia, "that the smart docs - including, I might add, one who doesn't even live in this town - think that all these folks who have been suffering at the hands of this witch in our midst are imagining it! Somewhere further on down the page you'll find a commentary by some journalist who has translated all this medic speak into plain English. He talks about people having panic reactions to fears that they might have caught something from someone else. Oh, and get this - the reason why most of the people affected are women is because we are more emotional and, he says, prone to this kind of reaction! I'll tell you, Betty, if I ever meet those smart asses, I will personally string them up!"

"It's ridiculous," said Betty. "How can you imagine being gassed?"

"How indeed, Betty my friend?"

"Things are getting more and more out of hand, Virginia. All that stuff's going to put one helluva big brake on whatever the police are trying to do. They might be trying but they have not achieved much and now they have the perfect excuse to do nothing!"

"Well, they might stop doing anything but I'll tell you - we are not!"

Several streets away, George had gone right round to Walter's house.

"Read this?" he said, throwing the newspaper on the table and reaching for a plum from the bowl nearby.

"Yes, I have," said Walter.

"And?"

"Well, do you think we imagined it?"

"Do I think we imagined it?!" said George, splurting half-chewed fruit on to the surface of the table. "I have never heard anything so ridiculous in my life. I surely hope you don't think so."

"No, of course not."

"One thing you can be sure of, Walt, is that this is not going to calm the spirits of the would-be witch hunters in our midst. Mark my words - good intentions the doctors may have but all this report will cause is more trouble!"

"I fear you are right, George."

"Let's be constructive, Walt. We and the other folks round here who have a semblance of having their heads screwed on properly have got to keep up our efforts. We have got to find who is doing all these horrible, nasty, wicked things to us all but also have to stop some, dare I say such a thing in the light of this report - emotional people - from taking the law into their own hands and doing something that they can only regret later."

"Gotcha, George."

"Let's go!"

From that morning on, the two men and the others of the watch party spent most of the daylight and nighttime hours wandering the streets, stopping only to sleep, feed and refresh with the occasional beer. Most of the twenty-four hours of each day were covered by the men taking their task in shifts but they realised that they were far too few in number to monitor the whole area all of the time. Nevertheless, after just three or four days, it seemed as if their efforts were worthwhile although not in the direction that any one of them would have preferred.

As usual, George and Walter were walking together, both still harbouring sufficient sense of unease at their earlier experience to deter them from being completely alone, at least for the whole of their time on the streets. Turning into Tuscola Avenue on a planned route that was now becoming established as a routine, they became aware of a cluster of lights on the street at the far end. Soon it became evident that the lights were being held by a group of people, all women, milling about in front of a house with an illuminated upstairs bedroom window.

"That's Annie Murphy's!" said Walter.

"Let's find out what's going on," said George, and they both quickened their pace.

As they hurried towards the group, two other men came running towards them.

"Come on, guys!" said one. "We've gotta stop this!"

"What's happening?" shouted Walter, as he and George followed the other two.

"Unless we do something," said one man turning his head back over his shoulder, "you are going to have the privilege of seeing a real-life lynch mob in action. They're after Annie Murphy. Come on!"

When they arrived at the house, the women were lined up, all facing the house and looking upwards. The random shouts and snippets of conversation that the men had witnessed from further away had settled and the group was largely silent, although most of them continued to shuffle on the spot; some had their hands on their hips. At the upstairs bedroom window stood another woman, clearly Annie Murphy. Her posture was bent slightly forwards with her hands resting on the window ledge. She was looking outwards towards the other women but her face was impassive, devoid of emotional expression. The men looked back and forth from the women in the street to the face at the window. *A stand-off, a major stand-off,* thought Walter.

It felt to the men as if they were standing on the brink of a tinder box, about to erupt in major conflagration at any moment and, for a few minutes, they felt paralysed in action. But then, when Virginia Adams made a more purposeful movement from the front of the crowd towards the house, George moved instinctively towards her and the other men followed.

"Stop it Virginia!" he said, grasping her gently but firmly with both hands on her shoulders and looking straight into her face. "Just stop it!"

"Stop what?" she said, almost with an air of surprise. "We haven't done anything yet."

"And I aim to keep it that way," said George.

"George, who do you think you are? If it was left up to people like you in this town, we'd all be cursed for a generation by this witch - or longer, if she's got any descendants like her. The police are bound by rules and cannot do anything so it's left to the common folk, like us here tonight, to rid the town of the menace once and for all. And that's precisely what we aim to do. Now get out of my way!" She began to push him aside and step towards the house but he held her back forcibly by one of her arms.

"And do you think the police are going to sit quietly by and ignore everything when you have gone about your business, committing who knows how many crimes in the process?   I don't think so! At best, you will end up in gaol; at worst you'll be fried in a chair."

"You know what, George, I don't care. I don't care because, if that's what it takes to get the Devil out of here, I am quite willing to sacrifice myself. And what happens if we do nothing? Sooner or later, at the hands of this bitch we will all end up dead or, dare I say it, even worse."

"OK, Virginia, if you and your lot don't care about yourselves, maybe you will care about this.   Supposing this woman is an agent of the Devil, how do you think he is likely to react when you take out one of his number? Lie back and say, ' OK, I guess they won after all'? No, he's going to unleash the whole of hell on the town! That guy down there could do a lot worse if he wanted to. Most of the time, in fact, he let's us go about our business - don't ask me why. Then sometimes he likes to play his dirty tricks but afterwards he goes away again until the next time. And that's what would happen with all this if you let it. Eventually, he would go away. But cross him deliberately and he's going to come back at us a thousand-fold. And this is the important bit: those that would be affected would not be just you and your crew but a whole load of other people who had nothing to do with your crazy ideas as to how to sort things out!"

Virginia was about to react but the crowd calmed. Betty, just to her side, was obviously touched by George's forceful but meaningful outburst. She gently clutched her neighbour's arm and looked tenderly into her face.

"Virginia, he makes a good point, I have to say. Supposing the worst will come of this." Virginia fell silent. Betty turned around. "Anna, what do you think?"

"I don't know what to think, Betty. I am now getting really confused. We all agreed that we are in this with Virginia and I hold to that, I really do," and, raising her voice, added, "and we will see it all through, we really will," and then, more quietly, "but just supposing George is right."

"We've got to be careful," shouted a woman from the back. The face from the window continued to stare abstractedly albeit perhaps with a calmer air.

"What's wrong with you all?" shouted Virginia back to the crowd. "Are we going to do this or aren't we?"

Several of the women moved forwards as if to follow Virginia towards the house but a number of the others shuffled nervously and looked at each other without speaking. George sensed the new lack of unity in the group and took his advantage. Shouting deliberately towards those at the back, who seemed the most hesitant, he said, "I know all of you ladies well. We have lived together in peace and harmony in this community for many years. I also know that you are sensible, thinking and caring and would not want to do anything unjust or that might backfire in a spectacular way. As your friend, I implore you to at least think; don't do anything hasty. We are all agreed, myself included, that we have to do whatever is necessary to clear up this town of whatever it is that has befallen it. But, above all, we must be sure that we don't simply make matters worse. So please think before you do anything!"

Virginia looked at the crowd, which had now become universally motionless. Initially, she did not speak but, after a minute or two, turned back towards George.

"Well, a fine speech, Mr. George Pearce," she said in measured tone. "But this is not the end of the matter. You may have scored a victory tonight but I tell you we will be back. And we will sort things out once and for all."

"OK," she said to the other women, "let's give it a rest for tonight. We'll make our plans for the next move later. Let's go!" She strode off back up Tuscola Avenue and the other women followed dutifully.

"It was a fine speech, actually, Mr. George Pearce," said Walter. "Congratulations."

"It just came out. I didn't think much about it. But thanks."

"Certainly did the trick, George."

"Sure - but for how long, I wonder."

"As long as that woman's in charge, I fear they'll be back," said Walter.

"Me too. I used to think she was such a nice person."

"I think she was, George, but circumstances change people."

"Seems so."

As the two men walked together down Tuscola Avenue towards the smaller side streets, the face at the illuminated bedroom window followed their movements until they turned a corner. Then the light went out.

For the next two weeks, the town was quiet. The men continued their daily rituals, monitoring the streets, but saw and heard nothing untoward. Devoid of new developments, the local newspapers did not mention the mystery gasser. There was no new medical or forensic evidence.

But Virginia continued to mobilise support for her would-be vigilante actions, if anything more determined following George's intervention on the street. Slowly but surely, she was bringing the women back to her point of view, recounting repeatedly the gruesome details of those who had fallen victim to the menace and particularly the "beautiful, innocent Robinson twin girls". The tactic was successful, especially since Mrs. Robinson was now virtually debilitated by constant anxiety and depression, despite the full recovery of her children, and served as an ongoing reminder of the possible longterm damage that could be done by "the witch in our midst" if she were allowed to get away with it.

And so the group reformed with a vengeance and a determination that this time nobody would be allowed to thwart their intentions. They planned their coup with much greater precision to minimise the risk of being interrupted. On the night, the women would disperse themselves in small groups of two or three around the streets neighbouring Tuscola Avenue, coming together as a larger body at Annie Murphy's house only at an exact, prearranged time. Use of lights would be avoided until the last minute, when all the women had congregated into one group, unless anyone saw somebody that might disrupt their plan. In that case, the woman would alert the others by turning on her light, extinguishing it when the danger had passed. If that occurred after the prearranged time, the women would gather together as soon as all lights were extinguished. Virginia and two other women would carry the tools necessary to enter the house, should Annie fail to answer the door. The one part of the plan that was not decided or even discussed in detail was what they were going to do once they had apprehended Annie Murphy, probably because most of the women did not want consciously to consider the possibilities and Virginia did not want to draw attention to them. In truth, though, Virginia herself was not entirely sure; she satisfied herself with the belief that everything would become obvious at the time; ideally Annie Murphy could be persuaded forcibly to leave the town of her own accord.

Towards the end of the two weeks following their first venture, the women were prepared. They were gathered in the darkness in small groups in the streets around Tuscola Avenue waiting for the moment to congregate and strike. Most of their contingency plans proved unnecessary because they saw no-one between arriving on the streets and the agreed time of execution of their plan. And, at that time, they all moved in concert, arriving virtually simultaneously at the front of Annie Murphy's house. Virginia had positioned herself at the front of the group.

But, on this occasion, the house was in darkness. Several of the women scanned around the upstairs bedroom with their eyes, looking for signs of life but saw none. Virginia, Betty and two of the other women took it upon themselves to look around the sides and back of the house but saw nothing. They hammered vigorously on the front door knocker, stepped back a few paces and waited for a minute or two. Receiving no response, they hammered again - no response.

"Right," said Virginia to the others, "now is the time to move!" She held up a crowbar to show the others and moved purposefully the few steps back to the door. With the skill of someone who might have used the tool many times before, which she had not, she succeeded in forcing the door in the space of a minute, assisted by Betty applying extra force to the crowbar handle for the last surge of effort. Virginia, still gripping her crowbar, turned on the hall light and the women flocked in, some spreading out into the downstairs rooms and others filing up the stairs to the upper rooms. But gradually, slowly, they all returned to the hallway; the house was empty.

"She's out on the street!" cried one of the women. "Let's go!"

"Wait!" said another. "We've been hanging around the streets round here for some time now and got no sight of her. I guess we'd have seen her if she was out there."

"Well, we've got to check," said Virginia. "Come on!"

They gathered back on the street and, under Virginia's direction, split into strategic groups to explore the area in military style so that their victim would be unable to escape through their ranks, should she try to. But when, as agreed, they reunited at Annie Murphy's one hour later, the mood was one of universal disappointment for, if Annie were on the streets, it was on none of those in their extended neighbourhood. Three of the women, including Virginia, volunteered to stay at the house overnight in case she returned.

The following morning, with the benefit of daylight, and still so sign of their target, they went over the house more thoroughly, searched the cupboards, drawers and wardrobes and discovered that all Annie's personal effects had been removed. The bird had flown the nest.

And so it continued. With unacknowledged mixed sentiments of disbelief, distrust and disappointment, the women repeated their exercise on each of the following two nights, supplemented by further searches of the streets during the day, before finally accepting that Annie Murphy was no longer in New Amboise. Although some of the women pointed out that her leaving the town was at least one of their intended goals, so high had run the bloodlust that it took some time before others came to terms with the fact that their prey had escaped her pursuers. But, by a week later, most had come to terms with their new-found situation and returned to their routine daily patterns of life.

"One thing I can now say for sure," said Betty, as she handed Virginia her coffee, "and in my heart I think we can take the credit for it, is that Annie Murphy is no longer in our midst."

"And thank the Lord for that!" said Virginia. "And not only that, Betty, but we have been proved right. Notice, if you will, that there have been no more gassings reported since that bitch - or, should I say more accurately, witch - has been forced out."

"I know. Now maybe we can all rest in peace again."

George and Walter were unsure whether their third drink within the hour was a token of celebration or dismay. But there they were, back as usual in their familiar bar with their familiar beer and none of that had changed.

"On the one hand," said Walter, "if that Annie Murphy was the cause of our troubles, well at least she has now gone but, on the other, I cannot say that I agree with the means those women used to bring it about. Neither do I much like the way they are now parading themselves around as the saviour of us all but you have to admit that, if they have rid our community of this menace, for that at least we have to be thankful. And what they say seems to be true; there have been no more gassings since Annie Murphy left town."

"That much is true, Walt. But can I also point out - and this is something the women would not want to hear - there were no gassings for two weeks before the women took their action and we know Annie Murphy was still in town then because we saw her. In fact, the gassings stopped pretty much around the time when that doctor suggested it was all in everybody's imagination."

"Well, it wasn't in ours, that's for sure."

"I guess not. But I wouldn't like to speak for the rest of the world. And, to be honest, so much has happened I'm not sure of anything any more."

And so, with the departure of Annie Murphy, coincidentally or not New Amboise settled back to a life of relative peace. The gassings ceased and none of those affected showed any lasting symptoms. The disruption to the town would never be forgotten but, the longer time passed with no recurrence, the more the anxieties of its residents eased, confidence grew and slowly the day-to-day business of the town returned to normal. Even Walter and George were ultimately able to share a drink together with a conversation that now reverted to its old pattern, including the baseball game, the local gossip and the inadequacy of the local government. Proud of their achievement in ridding the town of a menace, Virginia and her friends rested in self-satisfied glory and felt no need to discuss the matter further.

The New Amboise community would not know it but its contentment at restoring peace to their town did not mean that strange happenings had ceased completely everywhere and for ever. Over the years, outbreaks of widely different but universally unexplained illnesses occurred in several continents, mostly among teenage girls: chattering of teeth, uncontrollable laughter, trembling of limbs, rashes and cuts. And blackouts, as in an English Cotswold village.

Chapter 4

Combe Hollow Village, Gloucestershire, UK May 1998

"Come quickly, Mrs. Charles!   One of the girls has collapsed and we need your first aid skills."

Tina Charles glanced sideways towards the half-open classroom door, the space being filled with the anxious face of her colleague, staring towards her.

"Coming, Mrs. Stacey!   Girls, no doubt I shall be back soon," she said as she placed her book on her desk and moved towards the door. "In the meantime, do exercise six, which you will find at the end of the chapter we were just discussing." Half-heartedly, the students began to flick through the pages of the books on their desks as their teacher rushed out of the room.

Three doors down the corridor, Pam Stacey was already waiting at the entrance to her own classroom and hastily beckoned her colleague inside. They moved to opposite sides of a teenage girl, prostrate on the floor. Her eyes and mouth were open and still but her arms and legs were twitching erratically. As Tina took her arm to take her pulse, the girl tried to sit up and inhaled deeply but then the twitching increased and she slowly lay down again, exhaling as her body reached the ground.

"Her pulse is a bit fast but otherwise normal and she is obviously breathing OK," said Tina. "What happened?"

"She - sorry, I mean Alison - was standing at the front here, reading to the class - we had a short-story homework and some of the girls were chosen to read theirs to the others. There was a bit where Alison stumbled a bit in her reading out loud and one of the other girls laughed - very meanly, I might add," she said looking towards the class. "Then Alison stopped speaking altogether and started breathing heavily. After a few seconds, maybe longer, she sat down on the floor, then lay back and started twitching - like this."

"Actually, I think it's stopping now," said Tina, looking intently at the girl.

"What do you think?" said Pam. "Has she had a fit?"

"Well, maybe. I have seen fits before. I'm no expert but it's an odd one. Obviously we need the doctor fast."

"I've sent one of the girls to the office to call for him. If you're OK to stay here, I'll go and see what is happening."

"Yes, good idea."

Yes, thought Tina, I have seen fits before but none like this - except, that is, for the one yesterday. She tried hard to recall the similarities and differences between the two. They were all standing at the edge of the school field, along with the parents and visitors, watching the girls' competitions. A normal sports day in most respects. The girls in the round-the-field race were running fast but not that fast. As the leaders came down the home edge of the field, they passed a group of women spectators when the leading girl suddenly stopped and began breathing heavily. Tina had thought she was just out of breath but then the girl suddenly sat down and began twitching her arms and legs. She remained sitting for a minute or two before lying down, seemingly purposefully, onto her back. Her mouth and eyes stayed open but the twitching continued. After a couple of minutes, she exhaled deeply and sat up again. By the time Tina, as the first aid attendant, had reached her, the girl was awake and talking. Since she recovered rapidly, emergency medical attention was not thought necessary but she was advised to go home, rest and see her doctor the next day. Tina telephoned her parents to let them know what had happened. Strange coincidence, she thought. *A virus - or what?*

By the time the GP arrived, Alison was conscious again. Apart from seeming a little subdued, she seemed to have recovered completely. Completing his examination, the doctor seemed satisfied.

I don't find any evidence of anything urgent," he said, "but we will need to get a formal specialist opinion. I will refer her for an early appointment at the hospital. Has anyone else in the school been ill recently? I'm just wondering if there may be something infectious going around that could have precipitated this blackout. That is often the case - a virus or something like that."

Ah, as I thought, a virus, said Tina to herself. "Well, strangely enough, doctor, there was another girl yesterday who had a similar turn at our sports day. She was just running around the field with the others when she seemed to pass out. She recovered much more quickly though so we did not think it necessary to get an urgent medical opinion. We advised her to rest and see her own doctor as soon as possible."

"Thank you. Maybe it is a virus then although I have to say that Alison here doesn't have a raised temperature. Maybe it will come later. Did the girl yesterday have a temperature?"

"I'm sorry, doctor, I don't know. We didn't have a thermometer at the sports field."

"Not to worry. I will organise the referral to hospital and we will see what they have to say."

After the doctor had left and arrangements had been made to get the girl safely home, Tina and Pam were keen to return things to normal as soon as possible. The girl's parents were contacted and, pending their arrival, the girl was taken to a quiet room in the company of one of the other teachers. Tina returned to her class and Pam tried to resume work with her students. However, some of the girls in Alison's class remained quite agitated. The general mood was one of noisy chatter with some of the girls shifting aimlessly around in their seats.

"Come on, girls. Settle down now and let's just get on," said Pam. "This is nothing to worry about. These things happen sometimes."

"Will she be all right?" said one. "She was my friend and it is horrible seeing something like that happen to her. All that shaking - why was she doing that?"

It soon became clear that the girls' anxieties were not going to settle rapidly and the time for the lesson to finish was rapidly approaching. Tina therefore abandoned any further attempts to teach and took the remaining time to calm their fears and explain, as far as she could, the nature of blackouts, what may cause them and especially that they usually recover to leave no lasting effects.

"What about that girl at the sports day yesterday?" said another. "It looks as if she had got the same thing."

"Well, as the doctor told us, it may be a virus infection or something like that which has affected both of them. Or it could be just a coincidence. There is no point in our speculating, girls; we will find out when the doctors have done all their tests. In the meantime, as I said, there is nothing to worry about. I am sure they will both be fine."

"But what about us? If it's a virus, we might catch it and end up having horrible attacks like those," said one girl, crying.

The chiming clock marked the end of the lesson. As most of the girls left, Pam stayed behind for a few minutes to add a few more words of comfort to the two or three girls who seemed more distressed than most and then returned to the staff room for what she decided was a well-earned cup of coffee.

"Well, we don't often get visits from Public Health," said the headmaster, "but I admit it's a curious business and I am, of course, delighted to offer you as much help as I can."

"Thank you, Mr. Cartwright. It is much appreciated."

John Cartwright sat behind his desk, a position that always gave him a feeling of protection, while Dr. Soames and his assistant took their seats on the other side. The head's most trusted teachers sat in seats to the side.

"Let me summarise the situation as I understand it," began the doctor, "but please interrupt at any stage if you feel I am being inaccurate or indeed if you feel that you have anything at all to add."

"It appears," he continued, "that the present bout of illness - let's call it that for want of anything better at this stage - began in the school about ten days ago when one of the pupils collapsed whilst running in the sports-day events. The following day, a second girl had a similar attack in one of the lessons, as she was reading to the rest of the class. Since then, a total of thirty-two girls have become ill in similar ways. In all cases, it seems, the affected individual loses consciousness for a few minutes and develops twitching of the arms and legs."

"Some observers, based upon their own personal experiences, have suggested that the attacks are epileptic fits, which would not be an unreasonable conclusion. However, there are strange features to the whole business which, as yet, remain unexplained."

"Like what?" asked one of the teachers.

"Well, first, the attacks themselves are unusual for epilepsy. One or two of the teachers have wide experience of epilepsy, in one case for example because they have an afflicted daughter - not at the school - and they commented that the twitching is much more erratic and less forceful than in any of the fits that they have seen. And it is not just one case where this unusual behaviour has been observed; it seems that the pattern of the attacks was similar in all the cases, at least those for which we have good eye-witness reports."

"Secondly, and much more importantly, is why so many girls have had similar attacks over a relatively short time period. Two could be just a coincidence but for over thirty to have been affected indicates that we need to look for something that has caused them and that is principally why I am here."

"I don't need to bore you with too many medical technicalities but my team will be looking for something in the environment, in its broadest sense, by which I mean something in the air, the water, their food and so on - in short, anything that all those affected girls have come across and which we can implicate as a cause of their attacks. We cannot be sure when they would have been exposed to such a thing because we know that different triggers work over different time scales but it would be reasonable to state that it was probably within one week of the first girl's attack, if not much less."

"So, my question to you is whether anything has changed recently in the school - in their meals, the water supply, for example. And whether any work has been carried out - decoration, painting, plastering, any kind of refurbishment - within the school. Or in the grounds and fields, such as weed-killing, fertilisation - in short, anything you can think of."

The teachers agreed that nothing new had taken place within the school within the defined time period. One of the teachers stated that diet was unlikely to be responsible because at least two, if not three, of the afflicted girls were vegetarian and had different meals from the others. One even brought her own lunch with her and never ate the school meals. As for the grounds, no recent spraying or other treatment had taken place but they could not reliably comment on the fields that surrounded the school because they were under the direction of a neighbouring farmer.

Dr. Soames went on to explain that tests were underway on blood samples from the girls which hopefully would reveal the presence of any poisonous substances that they may have picked up from the area around the school, including agricultural pesticides, and which may have sparked off the attacks. In the meantime, he proposed to talk to the neighbouring farmer but there seemed little else to do until further evidence became available. He expressed his thanks to the staff and left.

"Well, it seems as if our Dr. Soames is on the case," said the headmaster, "and I have to say that his proposals sound very reasonable, at least to us as lay people. It appears that there is little more for us to do until we hear further from him. Naturally, you will all be vigilant not only for any other illnesses affecting the girls but also for any trigger of the types he mentioned that may be causing the attacks. Or hopefully I can say *that have caused the attacks* because they are now all in the past and we will see no more. So, unless anyone has anything else to add, I bid you all good morning."

Two days later, three girls from the school wandered into town during a free break from their lessons. They trod a familiar route to the collection of shops and cafes on the high street that, during the time available, could be reached and explored before a timely return to their next lesson. In mindless chatter, they ambled side by side, joking and giggling in the way that only teenagers can do. Carefree they seemed to be, intermittently tossing their hair and sometimes almost skipping. They were largely oblivious to their surroundings, only just avoiding colliding with the old man walking towards them and certainly not noticing the lady standing in a doorway gazing out towards the street. Greying, black hair and round rimless glasses decorated a round, motionless face; in company with an erect posture and arms folded across her chest, her whole demeanour seemed purposeless. Perhaps, therefore, it was hardly surprising that the girls gave her no second look.

But a teacher on the other side of the road, walking back to school in the opposite direction, did cast her a glance of recognition. Not that the woman's appearance was particularly striking but there was something about her that seemed familiar to Mrs. Stocks. *Where have I seen that woman before?* Having no reason to give it a second thought, she walked briskly on. About twenty yards further on, having now passed the woman and the girls, her attention was drawn back from where she had come by a loud scream. Turning her head, she saw two of the girls in obvious distress, gathered round the third girl, lying in the road. Her arms and legs were twitching but her face seemed composed and her eyes were open. A number of passers-by had also assembled to offer help but the lady with the greying hair and round glasses remained motionless in the doorway.

A fortuitous result of the spate of attacks at the school was that Mrs. Stocks now knew what to expect so she waited calmly, reassuring the others, until the twitching ceased and the girl regained consciousness. With someone knowledgeable and responsible now in control, most of the passers-by then drifted away except for one man who remained, taking photographs.

Just someone from the local newspaper, he explained, who happened to be on his way to another assignment when the girl fell ill. He had, of course, heard about the recent misfortune affecting a number of girls at the school and felt duty bound to keep his readers informed of the latest developments in this sorry tale. He wished all those affected well but declined the teacher's request not to publicise the matter further for reasons that he had already given, that it was in the public interest. Naturally, he would ensure that the girl could not be identified from any photographs that he used in his story. It became clear, despite further protestations from the teacher, that the journalist would not be swayed in his intent so she assisted the girl back to her feet and returned her to the school. She would check with the headmaster that the story could not be blocked but she did not hold out much hope and, anyway, the tragedy was, by now, becoming common knowledge in the village.

The following morning, on her way to work, she stopped off at the local newsagent for a copy of the newspaper. As was her custom, she settled at her desk with a cup of coffee before the morning's lessons began and flicked through the pages of the paper. *How will the hacks have distorted things this time?* she thought, remembering how a minor break-in to the corner classroom the previous year had somehow been translated as an affront to the girls' dignity and an obstacle to their educational progress when, in truth, all that had happened was the theft from a cupboard of a vacuum cleaner and a television that was hardly ever used.

Well, here are the photographs. She scanned the pictures and, yes, the journalist had been true to his word. A girl in school uniform could be seen lying in the road, surrounded by the other girls and passers-by but her head was turned away from the camera. Apart from being recognisable from the uniform as a member of their school, there were no other identifying features. The teacher's eyes roved over the other two pictures. Taken from the other side of the road, looking towards the shops, the angle was different but the content similar. And then she focussed on the details in the background. *There is that woman in the shop doorway whom I thought I recognised.*

She looked more closely for details to help jog her memory of where she may have seen her before. She certainly had a memorable face and stance, even though the features were not in themselves remarkable. *Yes, I remember now - it was at the school sports day! She was standing by the side of the field as the girls ran past. I remember seeing her because she was a member of the crowd of spectators close to where the girl collapsed.* Happy that her curiosity had been satisfied, she skimmed over the content of the article. Finding nothing to alarm her, indeed, she thought, nothing that was not already in the public domain, she took a sip of coffee and moved on to articles that she decided were more interesting and informative.

At the headmaster's instigation, a select group of teachers had been constituted to consider any new events, in particular any further attacks amongst the girls, to decide what, if any, new information this provided and any specific action that needed to be taken. Dr. Soames from Public Health had asked to be informed so it also made a forum for them to crystallise the information that they would pass on. The group met after each new happening and invited along eye witnesses. They met later in the morning the day after the girl's attack in the street and Mrs. Stocks was there.

"Well, I am very sorry to hear that we are not, after all, rid of this problem yet but I give you my congratulations on handling the situation so well," said the headmaster, after Mrs. Stocks had given her account.

"It wasn't difficult really," she replied, "because I recognised it as the same sort of attack that the others had had and knew that she would be fine. So I managed to stay calm - which is just as well; otherwise I might not have been so patient with that journalist."

"Was he the one that wrote today's article in the Star?" asked one of the other teachers.

"Yes, but fortunately - and I hope you agree - it doesn't seem to have done too much damage," replied Mrs. Stocks. "Well, to be honest," she continued, "personally I didn't think it was news at all. But maybe that's what sells newspapers - lack of news!" A ripple of laughter ran through the group.

"He also assured me it would not be possible to identify the girls from his photographs and he seems to have held to that."

"Yes, indeed," said Pam Stacey, holding a copy of the newspaper. "That is good. In fact, the only person who could possibly be identified from the detail in the pictures is that woman standing in the doorway," she added, holding up the paper at the relevant page for the others to see, "but hopefully she would not mind."

"I think it is only minors for whom one has to preserve anonymity without permission" said John Cartwright. "If adults are caught on camera in a public place, it's too bad."

"I recognise that woman," said one of the group, leaning forward to examine the photograph. "She was one of a group of middle-aged women, perhaps three or four, huddled together in a group, watching the sports day. I remember it because at the time I thought it was a bit unusual to see a group of women like that. Not that there is anything wrong with it - and I am glad that our school activities appeal to the broader community - but it seemed obvious that they didn't have any daughters or granddaughters in the races - there was no-one in particular that they were cheering for. That's why they stood out."

"That's Megan Askew!" said Mrs. Stocks. "She lives in a small cottage right at the far end of the village. Mind you, I am not surprised that you do not know her because very few people do. She usually keeps herself to herself and hardly ever seems to go out although I think she does talk to her neighbour. But then you probably wouldn't know that either because her neighbour is a fairly lonely soul too! And more recently, she's taken to spending time at the Black's farmhouse but you still don't see her much because she stays indoors all the time. She moved into the village about six months ago. Actually, I am surprised to see her out in the village and especially at the sports day but then maybe she is just very shy and has taken some time getting used to being here. Maybe she's just gradually branching out."

"How do you know her?" said one.

"Well, I don't know her at all really but I found out she had come to the village when I went round with the leaflets for the local elections. I called at all the houses. She answered the door - didn't say much, mind you - what I picked up was from her neighbour. But I do recognise her."

"Well," said the headmaster, interrupting any further conversation, "it is good that our neighbours are keen to support us. Does anyone have anything to add to what we have concluded about the latest attack amongst the girls? If not, I suggest we call the meeting closed. Naturally, as I have said on previous occasions, I hope we do not need to meet again except to draw an end to the matter but, if anything untoward does arise, please let me know and we will reconvene."

Dr. Soames surveyed the fields as he walked towards the farmhouse from the parking area by the road and, as he got closer, the farm machinery parked haphazardly in the yard. He dodged amongst the chickens running free, whilst simultaneously trying to avoid the piles of excrement littered across the old stone paving. A cockerel was standing on one of a group of plastic butts at the far end of the yard, presumably containing farm chemicals.

The farmhouse was old and traditional, perhaps dating from the late eighteenth or early nineteenth century, he thought, but it was not well maintained. The stone roof slates were cracking; paint was peeling from the window frames; and the gaps between the eaves and the walls would have been no obstruction to a westerly wind. *I think I am going to find a damp house,* he thought.

He did not need to knock because, as he approached the house, the door was opened by a ruddy-faced, unshaven man, shabbily dressed in an old, black t-shirt, heavily stained overalls and dirty black boots. He was slightly overweight; his hair was wavy and early greying, not recently cut, cascading across his forehead but with early balding over the crown. His eyes were bloodshot; as the doctor got closer, it was evident the farmer was smelling of alcohol.

"Yes?" he said brusquely.

Dr. Soames introduced himself and, after some persuasion, was allowed by the farmer into his sitting room. The doctor sat down on the chair that he perceived to be cleanest and explained that he was investigating the mysterious attacks that had affected a number of girls at the neighbouring school and which, so far, defied explanation.

"And what's that got to do with me?" said the farmer.

"Well, sir," began the doctor. "Actually, before I go on, do you mind if you tell me your name? It would be so much easier to refer to you by name, if you do not find that too intrusive."

"Arthur Black."

"Well, Mr. Black, we know from previous attacks of this kind that sometimes they can be caused by chemical poisoning."

"And what's that got to do with me?" said the farmer. "I don't go around deliberately poisoning people. Mind you, I can think of some who might help us all by taking a good dose of poison."

"I am sure you do not deliberately poison people, Mr. Black. That did not even cross my mind. No, I am here because some chemicals used on the farm are known to produce attacks like these if they are ingested into the human body. May I ask if you have recently been doing any crop spraying or other kind of treatment to the land that uses chemical substances? I am not suggesting that you have done anything wrong - this is not a blame game - I am merely trying to get to the bottom of this matter."

"Well, of course I have!" replied Arthur Black. "I'm a farmer and it's that time of year, isn't it? You may not know much about farming in your hospital or wherever you work but I expect you know that that's what we do. Otherwise, you wouldn't be here, would you?" The farmer gave a self-satisfied grunt and slid slightly further down his chair in a gesture of indifference to the seeming authority of the doctor.

"That is true, Mr. Black, but what I need to know is when you last did some spraying."

The doctor began to see for the first time since his arrival the invisible effects that chronic, heavy alcohol consumption had had on his interviewee because Arthur Black was now clearly having difficulty remembering what had happened over the previous few days. Specifically, he had no idea when he last did any spraying although he thought it must have been recently because "that's what I do."

Apart from failing to recall what he did and when, it became immediately clear to the doctor that the effects of the farmer's alcoholic lifestyle on the brain were likely to have affected not only memory but also judgement. *Was he in the right frame of mind to be sure that the doses of the chemicals he was using were correct and that he had not inadvertently delivered to the atmosphere an excessive and probably toxic dose?*

Dr. Soames knew that the results of the blood tests were now critical because all would be explained if, as he suspected, the girls showed excessive levels of the toxic chemicals in their bloodstreams. However, he must ensure that the laboratory was looking in their tests for all potential poisons.

"Are you able to tell me which chemicals you use on your land, Mr. Black? If you cannot remember, do not worry but I would ask if I could examine the containers myself to establish what is in them. I could not help but notice some vats of chemicals in the yard on my way in. Would those be the ones you would use?"

"Yes, I keep them all out there. Sorry but, no, I cannot remember the names."

The farmer had become noticeably more quiescent and was now slightly slumped in the chair, almost staring at his knees. Dr. Soames was concluding that the unknowing propagator of community poisoning was falling asleep from his own form of self-poisoning when the farmer looked up and spoke:

"It's not so easy now I'm on my own. I have to work out everything for myself and do it all myself. Sometimes it's too much. Joan used to help me, you see - quite a lot really."

"Joan?" prompted the doctor, already suspecting the answer.

112

"Joan - my wife. She died towards the end of last year. Well, we assume she died; she's never been found."

"Never been found?" said the doctor with undisguised astonishment. "So how do you know she has died."

"That was the conclusion of the police. She was recorded as a missing person for a while - well, I suppose still is technically - but they never found her. I think they tried pretty hard. In the end, they decided that, since they couldn't find her alive anywhere, she must have died. Although, if she did, God knows how or where."

The doctor did not want to probe too much the probably distressed mind of a man he had only just met, and that was not the prime purpose of his visit, but he could not resist being immediately gripped by what sounded like a very disturbing story. And it seemed as if this was one thing that the farmer actually wanted to talk about.

"But she could be anywhere!"

"Probably not far away," said Mr. Black. "She couldn't drive and she hated buses and trains. Somebody could have driven her somewhere but she wouldn't have gone willingly because she didn't know anybody outside of the area. In fact, she never really went out of the house except sometimes to help on the farm a bit."

"Sorry to say this, Mr. Black, but do the police think she was murdered?"

"They don't know. No suspects. No evidence. No - what do you call it? - motive."

Dr. Soames tempered his initial inquisitiveness. "Extraordinary," he said. "I am so sorry, Mr. Black. If there is anything I can do, do not hesitate to let me know. In my line of work, I deal a lot with public bodies, including the police, and I am willing to look into it a bit, even if only maybe to give you some clearer answers."

"Thanks."

That is truly bizarre, thought Dr. Soames There seemed nothing much else useful to be said so he took his leave and concentrated on the main reason for his visit. He walked over to examine the chemicals in the farmyard. The vats had lids but were not sealed so the odour of rotten eggs obviously coming from at least one of the vats was unmistakeable as he got closer. *That's parathion,* he said to himself. The writing on the vats was weathered but sufficiently clear to confirm his suspicions as he examined the side of one of them. *Well, that would do for a start.*

Something prompted him to go back and question Mr. Black. Initially, he thought he would fail in his efforts because he gained no response from repeated knocking on the farmhouse door. He was about to give up and return to his car when the door opened to reveal the farmer, possibly smelling even more strongly of alcohol than before.

"Now what do you want?" he blurted.

Well, at least he recognises me. "Just one or two more questions if I may, Mr. Black. I don't need to come in." *Hopefully, he has forgotten our previous conversation already so may be willing to answer some questions about the chemicals without getting distressed.*

"What do you want?"

"I notice that you have a supply of the pesticide, parathion, in the yard. Is that something you may have sprayed recently?"

"Probably. It's spring, isn't it?"

"I just wanted to be sure without jumping to conclusions. The reason I am so keen is that parathion is a chemical known to cause blackouts in people - amongst other side effects - so it would be a good contender as the cause of the girls' attacks if you have sprayed it recently. As I said earlier, there is no blame attached; I just need to find out what has happened."

In a moment of clear thinking, the farmer responded: "Well, if that's so, how come they've never had them before when I have been using the stuff in the spring for years?"

The doctor fell silent for a few minutes while the farmer continued to stare at him. *Well, that is a good point, I must say. It cannot be anything to do with a particular susceptibility of these girls because they have all been at the school for a number of years and would certainly have come across the spray in a previous spring. It has to be something to do with the dose and his confusion; he must have got it wrong this year.*

"Mr. Black, can you be sure that the dose of parathion that you sprayed this year is the same as in previous years? Is there any possibility, however caused, that you could have given more this time?"

"No. We just go round with a standard tankful."

The possible means for Mr. Black's confusion to cause a problem cascaded one after another through Dr. Soames' mind: forgetting that the spraying had been done recently so that he repeated it unnecessarily and hence at more than the usual frequency; if the chemical had to be diluted, getting the dilution wrong; spraying areas that he would not usually and maybe closer to the school; and so on. It was clear that he would not get the answers to these possibilities by questioning the farmer any further. Suffice it to say that he had found a potential toxic chemical that had recently been sprayed on the land adjacent to the school and a reason, in the form of the farmer's alcohol-induced confusion, to explain how the dose administered this year was more toxic than in previous years. All he had to do now was to check all the other chemicals in the farm, ensure that parathion and any other toxins were amongst those being searched for in the girls' blood samples and then await the results of the tests.

"No, Dr. Soames, I cannot say, in all honesty that I have noticed," said the headmaster. "We are, of course aware of the various farming activities that go on nearby; that is one of the features, indeed usually the delights, of being a school in a rural community. In fact, we try to get the pupils to take an interest in what is going on as part of their broader education. So we do notice the crop spraying, although we may not know exactly what is being sprayed, but as for there being anything unusual about it this year, I cannot say there has. Let us ask the rest of the staff for their observations but personally I do not think it has occurred any more often than in the past or any closer to the school. If you do think the spraying is responsible, maybe the wind has carried the chemical towards us more this year - we have had a lot of south-westerly winds this spring which would blow over the farm towards the school."

"You are quite right, Mr. Cartwright; that could be an explanation. Unfortunately, there are too many imponderables, too many possibilities that cannot easily be addressed, such as the effects of Mr. Black's confusion. We may just have to wait for the blood test results but unfortunately the laboratory is not very speedy in analyses of this kind - they do not get asked for this type of investigation very often and have to set it up specially."

"Ah, Arthur Black - poor fellow!" said the headmaster.

"Yes," said the doctor, grasping the opportunity to satisfy his curiosity, "what do you make of all that? He told me his wife had disappeared and I assume he has taken to drink as a result. Sorry, I hope I am not speaking out of turn."

John Cartwright repeated the story of Mrs. Black's disappearance in an essentially similar way to that related by the farmer and nodded his head vigorously in agreement at every surprising facet of the misadventure highlighted by the doctor.

"Very strange indeed - I agree," concluded the headmaster. "It just seems that one day she disappeared off the face of the earth. Officially, she remains on the missing persons' register. The suggestion that she has been murdered is a little conjectural but the police raised it as a strong possibility - together with abduction from the vicinity - because any other explanation seems even less likely, when account is taken of the kind of person she was and the community in which she lived."

"I don't want to take on the role of a detective," said Dr. Soames, "but couldn't her husband have done it? There's a lot of land in which to dispose of her."

Mr. Cartwright shrugged his shoulders. "Maybe - but no evidence and no motive. They got on very well together - very well indeed. In fact, you would rarely see them apart. It was a very close family, the two of them and their daughter. If Mr. and Mrs. Black did leave the farm, which wasn't often, they were always together - literally. At harvest suppers and occasions like that when they did turn up, she would remain at his side throughout the whole occasion. The only time one of them left the house alone was when he was working on the land; she would then remain in the house. Sometimes, she would help him on the farm but, even then, she did not seem to be too far away from him."

"So presumably that is why he has taken to drink which, in turn, has made him rather muddled, shall we say?" said the doctor.

"Yes, indeed - although, in retrospect, some people who knew the family better than most believe that he was showing signs of being unwell for a year or two before she disappeared. Nothing too serious - just the odd lapse of memory, really - but enough to make people notice because it was unusual for him; he used to be a very organised person."

"In what ways, in particular?"

"Oh, everything really. The farm ran like a military machine with a strict timetable for the year; everything had a place and was in its place; his documents were all up to date and filed assiduously. Rumour even has it that he made his first will when he was twenty-nine and has reviewed it annually ever since; he's now sixty-three!"

"Does he have a large family?"

"His parents both died in a motor accident about four years ago. I'm sure that wouldn't have helped his mental state although they were not that close emotionally; they ran another farm about a mile or two away but Arthur didn't see them very often. They all functioned rather independently. Arthur doesn't have any brothers or sisters. As I said, he has a daughter - just the one - Jennie, who now works as a teaching assistant at the primary school in one of the villages a few miles away."

"Did she get on with both her parents?"

"Yes. She lived at home until quite recently and was very close to both of them. Her mother doted on her and was very protective towards her - too much, some would say. She rarely let her out of her sight, even when her daughter got into her late teens, and, I must say, Jennie didn't seem to object. In fact, I think she cherished the close relationship. And it seemed to work; they certainly looked after each other."

"So why did she leave?"

"Nobody is quite sure but she still calls in most Sundays on her own - she's not married. And the rest of the week, Arthur is fortunate in having Megan, who spends most of her time there now and seems to be very helpful to him. She and Jennie also seemed to get on very well together. In fact, I think it was through Jennie that Megan got to know her father."

The headmaster suddenly drew himself straight in the chair. "Anyway," he continued, "all that is not the primary reason for our getting together and I am conscious that it may now be me who is speaking out of turn. I trust that you will keep this aspect of our conversation confidential."

"Of course," replied the doctor. "I am sorry to have pursued it. It is just that it all seemed so strange when Mr. Black told me how his wife had suddenly disappeared."

"Yes, indeed," said Mr.Cartwright, "but I fear we may never obtain the answers."

Two women were huddled together in tub chairs around an open fire, from which the red glow of the coals stood out in contrast against the generally dark, unlit interior of the cottage. Flickers of flame from the fire cast occasional brief flashes of light across the lower face of the woman seated closest to it. One of the women, with greying black hair and round rimless glasses, sat upright with arms folded, looking hawk-like; she spent most of the time staring at the fire, even when she was speaking to her associate. The other, much more mouse-like, remained slightly bent at the waist with her hands in her lap.

"I like an open fire, don't you?" said the mouse. "Some of the people in the village think it's unnecessary at this time of year but I don't care. Anyway, you like it don't you?" she said to the other.

"Yes," was the simple reply.

This simple kind of banter continued for another ten minutes or so, during which the mouse frequently smiled and the more austere of the two looked bored or at least impassive. Sensing the other's lack of involvement, the former then made a conscious effort to move the conversation to something more serious.

"What do you think about all this business at the school, then?"

"Which business?" said the hawk.

"You know, all those blackouts that the girls have been having. I can't help wondering what could possibly have caused it. It must be something serious to have affected so many. I heard there were over twenty girls who had had the attacks," said the mouse.

"Thirty-two," said the other.

"So what do you think?"

"I think they are a lot of silly girls who are probably getting what they deserve."

"Deserve? How come? Deserve for what?"

120

"What people don't realise is that things they do in this life can have consequences, if not always to themselves then certainly to others. The world doesn't just sit around watching. Do something and you may find that it backfires, maybe not immediately but perhaps some time later - maybe quite a long time later," said the hawk, staring into the fire.

"So are you saying that what has happened to these girls is because of something that they have done wrong in the past? That sounds a bit harsh. In fact, it sounds like something you might hear from some of the more extreme members of the church. I can think of some in this village who might think like that but I am surprised to hear it come from you. Anyway, what could thirty-odd girls all have done to deserve the same punishment?" asked the other, visibly puzzled and holding her hands out in front of her.

"I did not say it was punishment as such. Just the consequence of somebody doing something silly. It might not be their fault but they happen to be the ones who get the backlash - someone has to. If it can't be the original perpetrator, then it falls on them."

"Sorry, Megan, but that sounds like a lot of mumbo-jumbo to me. If it's God taking revenge, then it's a funny god that would punish someone for something done by somebody else. It's not the idea of God that I was brought up with."

"I didn't say it was God. Elsie, there are things in this world and beyond that most people do not understand."

"Like what?" said Elsie.

"Forces, sometimes dark forces that do not care who they act against as long as their desires are fulfilled. You cannot ignore them."

"Oh Megan, please! I've heard that the powers-that-be here on earth are investigating whether Arthur Black may have poisoned the girls - not deliberately, of course, but by mistake. He is a bit muddled these days and it seems to me that he could quite easily have spread chemicals into the school without realising. Isn't that much more likely than your ideas about 'dark forces' as you call them?"

"Well, let's wait and see."

There was something symbiotic about the relationship between the two women. Elsie acted as a sounding board for Megan's pent-up emotions and, although she might disagree with what was said, Elsie took on the subservient role to her dominant partner. And, being a naturally shy, withdrawing and, to a degree, non-coping character, profited in some way from the control that Megan exerted over her. Their regular meetings seemed to work for both of them and they both knew that whatever was said between them would never be repeated outside of those four walls.

"You were in town the other day, weren't you?" said Elsie. "Did you see that girl have a do in the street. I read about it in the Star."

"As a matter of fact, I did," said Megan.

"How exciting!" said Elsie who, living most of the time in a part of the world where excitement was not a major feature, was easily aroused. "What did you think?" she added, beaming.

"Well, I wouldn't describe it as exciting," said Megan. "It was just like the others. If you remember, I was at the school sports day when that girl had the first attack."

"Oh yes! I had forgotten that."

"Actually," continued Megan, in a more hurried voice, "it was a bit more interesting this time because the farmer, Arthur Black, was on the street about the same time. In fact, the girls nearly knocked him over."

"So what?" said her friend. "Don't tell me he was crop spraying in the High Street!" and she burst into uncontrollable giggles.

"No, Elsie, he wasn't," said Megan with a sigh. "I've no idea why he was there. It just seems a strange coincidence now you mention about him and the crop spraying. Maybe it's not just the chemicals that he's used to affect them. Maybe he has other means as well. Like many people."

"Such as what?" said the other with unusual forcefulness. "Are you suggesting he is deliberately up to no good? And, if he is, how exactly do you suggest he caused the girl to black out in the street? The chemicals I can just about understand but what are you saying he managed to do in the middle of the village high street to cause a passer-by to have a fit?"

"Elsie, as I said before, there are dark forces around that you cannot detect. You have to admit it's a strange coincidence."

"Well, a coincidence is about all it seems to be. Arthur lives in the village; he is perfectly entitled to go into the High Street without necessarily being up to mischief. He's probably been there a thousand times and you wouldn't have suggested that he had caused any problems then."

"Actually, he rarely goes out now."

"Anyway," continued Elsie, "there were probably many other people in the High Street that you could implicate when the girl blacked out because they were there at the time and also had some kind of connection with the school. You, for instance!" And she laughed.

"I don't spray chemicals," said Megan. "Also, you forget that I know Arthur Black quite well."

"You know his daughter," said Elsie. "I don't know whether that automatically means that you know him that well."

Megan had become well acquainted with Arthur Black's daughter, Jennie, since they met at a charity auction soon after Megan's arrival in the village eight months earlier. Jennie had given to the auction, on behalf of her father, a basket of wild garlic grown on the farm. Megan was the successful bidder. They got into conversation as they were settling the payment at the end of the auction and, sensing an ease in each other's company, met for coffee on a few occasions afterwards. They soon formed a close bond. Their relationship grew even closer when Jennie's mother mysteriously disappeared a couple of months later; Jennie found a receptive ear for her outpourings of mixed emotions and confusion and Megan, for her part, managed to say just the right things at the right time to generate at least a temporary peace in the mind of her new-found friend.

Megan learned that Jennie had a mixed relationship with her father but got on better with her mother. In fact, the two were very close and depended on each other. The commonality of grief between the father and daughter had no doubt helped to improve their relationship but Jennie had major concerns for the future. It was clear that her father was not capable of running a large farm without his wife's support; indeed it was only then that she realised for the first time how much organisation had been put in by her mother over the years, even before her father began to show the early signs of dementia.

Jennie's father made it clear that he would like his daughter to take over the running of the farm when he was no longer capable and particularly when he had departed this earth, which he said, in one of his worst moments of grief, may be sooner rather than later. He stressed that the farm had been in the family for four generations and he had no desire to see that situation change. He realised that she may feel that the job should be done my a man but she was their only child and, as he put it, these days women do much the same work as men do. Naturally, if she agreed, the farm would be left to her in his will and he would trust her not to sell it out of the family. The future of the family farm depended on the continuing input from Jennie. She vowed that she would ensure never to leave the farm abandoned.

Contrary to Elsie's implication, Megan did also, by now, know Arthur Black quite well, partly through conversations with Jennie, but also, on a more personal level, because Megan increasingly accompanied her in visits to her father. The rather cold nature of part of their earlier relationship had led Jennie sometimes to feel nervous when alone in her father's company and Megan provided the perfect buffer between them. Although Megan chose not to employ her social skills in the company of Elsie, she was able, when required, to produce a side of interest and compassion. As a result of this quality, Arthur had come to accept her as a trustworthy companion of his daughter and engaged her freely in the conversations; indeed, he had come to quite like her. For Jennie, Megan's skills as mediator led to a warming of feelings between father and daughter; despite the past, Jennie was grateful because a close relationship with her Dad is what she would really always have liked but seemed to escape her. And Megan got closer to the family unit as well.

Over the months, Arthur, Jennie and Megan settled to become a close functioning unit. They met regularly at Arthur's farm, initially each week but increasingly often as time went by. Usually, they would take seats in the same positions to form a small circle around a coffee table. There they would discuss trivial day-to-day matters and memories from the past as well as the more serious issues concerning the present and future running of the farm. But they remained insular, seeming not to need the company of others or an environment different from Arthur's sitting room. It was perhaps not surprising then that Elsie had no awareness of Megan's knowledge of Arthur.

On one occasion, Arthur had a fall in the bathroom but Jennie was not available to attend urgently because she herself had been laid low by what was presumed to be a flu-like illness; she was confined to bed with muscle aching and shivering. Megan came to the rescue by going round to Arthur's home, heaving him into bed and calling the emergency doctor. After that successful intervention, Jennie often rested on Megan's generosity by asking her to visit her father alone if she had had to go out, particularly as his demands increased in concert with his worsening frailty. All three were in little doubt that the overall programme worked well and that a workable solution had been found to the inevitable emotional turmoil that followed the disappearance of Mrs. Black. And the relationship between Megan and Jennie grew closer as a result.

"Well, trust me," said Megan to Elsie, "I also know him well."

Dr. Soames walked into the makeshift office that had been provided for him in the village library for the period of his investigations in the locality. He enjoyed it - such a change from the starchy atmosphere of the University buildings in the city, where everyone had their own agenda and the search for truth sometimes took second place to a vying for position. He enjoyed walking up the stairs from the entrance in the village square, passing the shelves of books and the early bookworms seated at the tables dotted around the large upstairs reading room. So normal, so natural, so peaceful. Often, before passing into the comfortable albeit functional office at the end of the room, he would pause to examine the collection of books: local history of nearby villages, autobiographies of media-boosted celebrities and travel guides for the few who chose to venture outside their county.

This morning, his eyes were caught by a large leather-backed volume seated upright at the far end of a shelf close to his office: *Documented Local Ghost Stories*. As he lifted it from its position and flicked open the pages, it was clear that the book was a hand-made collection of stories, some typed, some hand-written, obviously put together by a keen amateur enthusiast. He vowed to read it in detail when he could justifiably find time away from his more pressing obligations.

As part of his usual morning routine, he took a coffee from the machine in the reading room, kindly turned on by the volunteer library staff on their arrival for the library's opening that day. *Not a posh Italian thing; just a cheap coffee maker but better than nothing,* he thought. He picked up the polystyrene cup from the opening at the bottom and walked into his room where the early sun's rays were cascading across the walls from the south-easterly facing window and settling on his desk. The bright light seemed to create a focus around the small pile of letters that constituted his first task of the day: dealing with the morning mail.

Following his usual routine, he took a mouthful of coffee and, while still standing, flicked through the collection of envelopes in the hope that that day's mail would include a letter from someone interesting for a change. So established was he in his work pattern and organisation that not only did he almost know who would write to him each day but also what they would have to say. However, when his eyes spotted one easily recognisable envelope, he put down the coffee and sat down with a frisson of excitement and a half smile.

At last, he thought as he opened the envelope, *now we have the proof we need.*

The report from his department was much briefer than most; Dr. Soames waved the single sheet of paper in the air and looked again in the envelope in the belief that he must have missed something. But no; he read the single sheet which explained that blood samples from all of the affected girls willing to provide a specimen had been sent to the Toxicology Unit of Imperial College, London, where scientists had carried out tests to determine the blood levels of all the common herbicides and pesticides used in the UK, including, at Dr. Soames' specific request, parathion. More time was required than would normally be the case because of the comprehensive nature of the search and because some of the investigations were conducted only rarely and had to be set up specially.

He flicked through the rest of the preamble and settled on the paragraph headed "Conclusion" at the foot of the page. He read it through three times. *Impossible!* he said to himself. *Just impossible!* Dr. Soames ignored the rest of the post and picked up the phone. He then sat at his desk for a few moments in thought before leaving the office.

On his way out, his attention was again caught by the leather-backed book on one of the shelves. Deciding he had time to spare following his phone calls before his next activity began, he took the volume from the shelf and settled at one of the reading desks.

It's good to have a distraction sometimes; it clears the mind, he decided. The collection was probably put together by an amateur local historian, he concluded, with information gleaned partly from documented references, mostly local newspapers, but a great deal also from local gossip. The author had clearly added his interpretations to the evidence, no doubt with some embellishment, but, since the prime aim was presumably to entertain and attract interest amongst the locals, that seemed to matter little.

The doctor skimmed through the several stories about haunted houses in the area's villages. As was usual with such tales, he noted, the evidence seemed largely to revolve around unexplained noises or lights in old properties for which an explanation simpler than the supernatural seemed more plausible. Occasionally someone had reported seeing something more tangible but generally little more than a vague shape in the shadows. One young girl reported seeing and was able to describe well a ghost in the corner of her bedroom; the vision was of a young adult woman dressed in eighteenth-century clothes with a whitened face and powdered wig. He could not resist a wry smile when he read later in the section, apparently written without any sense of irony, that three months later the girl was confined to a mental hospital.

Towards the end of the book was a section entitled "Other Unexplained Mysteries." *Just a quick look before I go*, he thought. He turned over "The Plague of Toads", "Lightning Strikes Twice in the Same Place" and "The Monster Hole in the Football Field" to reach a page entitled "Epidemic of Blackouts at a Country Fair". The flicking of his fingers came to an abrupt halt and he stared intently at the page.

He read slowly: "One of the strangest happenings in this region took place in 1984 in the village of Churnford. Every year, the locals organised a country fair, typical of those of many small communities throughout the country, and took over a large field adjacent to the old manor house for a day's entertainment. Numerous stalls were dotted around the periphery, selling anything from bric-a-brac to home-made cakes. In the centre of the field, people could take part in a number of traditional old English country games, such as skittles, hoop-la and bat-the-rat."

"At one edge of the field was a brass band, which played old folk tunes. Most years, the fair used a band from another nearby village but this year it was decided to allow children from local schools to display their talent. As it happened, a number of schools had got together six months or so before the fair to form an interschool brass band society and it was agreed that they would play at the fair. The children, in truth teenagers, were said to be a little nervous about playing in public but were keen and mostly looking forward to the opportunity."

"On the morning of the fair, the weather was overcast but the clouds cleared about mid-morning. The sun came out and it became warm but not unduly hot. The attendance was good and everyone seemed to be enjoying themselves. Some had even taken to dancing to the music played by the band."

"All went well until about three o'clock in the afternoon when, in the middle of playing one piece, a girl trumpeter suddenly stood up, dropped her instrument and collapsed to the ground, apparently unconscious. Fortunately, she came round after a few minutes and, although she was not well enough to continue playing, seemed largely to recover with no lasting consequences. No-one was too worried at this stage because, after all, one was used to young people fainting and usually it did not signify anything seriously wrong. However, it was not long before all that changed."

"About forty-five minutes after the first girl fainted, another trumpeter, who had been sitting very near the first girl, also stood up suddenly and blacked out. A coincidence? Possibly, were it not for the fact that over the next two hours a total of fifteen teenagers, about half the membership of the band, had also had similar attacks! Fortunately, each one seemed to regain consciousness quickly and none seemed any the worse for wear, except for feeling generally shaken and nervous."

"Over the next few weeks, all the affected teenagers, fourteen girls and one boy, were examined by doctors and nothing was found to be wrong. They even had a set of extensive tests but all turned out to be normal. The best that they could come up with was that it was some sort of "nervous reaction" that spread among the group."

"So it was all a mystery and remains so until this day. But I can vouch for the authenticity of this story because, although I was not there personally, I have spoken at length with one of the eye witnesses from the day and she is in little doubt as to what happened."

Not exactly a scientific text, thought Dr. Soames, *but compelling nevertheless. A nervous reaction? Well, maybe I suppose.*

Two days later, he was back at the school in the headmaster's office with the usual group of teachers selected to assist with the project. The meeting had been called specially by the doctor so the group was apprehensive to hear the news.

"I am sorry to have to tell you," said the doctor, "but the results of the blood tests are surprising, to say the least. None of the affected girls showed any trace in their blood of any of the pesticides, herbicides or other farm chemicals that are commonly used in this country. I say commonly but the laboratory also tested for lesser used ones and also other toxic substances and those results were also negative. It therefore seems very unlikely that the attacks were caused by poisoning from nearby farmland, whether that be Arthur Black's land or indeed anywhere else."

"But you decided that poisoning was the cause!" said one of the teachers.

"It was the most likely hypothesis, based on the evidence. Now that hypothesis has been discounted, we have to think of other possibilities."

"Like what?" said two or three of the group, in unison.

"As part of their all-embracing investigations, the laboratory did a number of other tests, including blood levels of the common hormones, that is the chemicals produced by the glands within our bodies. Most of them were normal but many of the girls showed abnormally high levels of cortisol. That is a hormone produced by the adrenal glands, which often rises in response to stress. Now, of course, it is possible that the stress we are talking about was simply the attack itself; in other words, the blackout caused a stress reaction, which led to an outpouring of cortisol from the adrenal glands and hence a rise in the level in the blood. But perhaps we should also consider whether the cortisol rise, whatever caused that, was itself responsible for the attacks - or even that something caused a stress reaction, which itself resulted simultaneously in a blackout and a rise in the level of cortisol in the blood."

"Sorry, you have lost me," said the headmaster, "and, dare I say, some of my colleagues too. But from the last thing you said, it seems you are suggesting that the attacks were all caused by stress. Am I right?"

"Stress in the broadest sense of the word, sir. Something yet undefined that stressed their bodies at that moment and caused them to black out. The raised hormone levels are simply a reflection of that reaction. What is odd is that, in some of the girls, the levels remained raised, even though the blood sample was taken several days after their attack."

"Could the poison not also have left the body by then?" said one of the teachers.

"No; the poison would have lingered in the body and also some of the girls gave blood samples very soon after their attack; there was no poison in any of their samples either. The stress hormone cortisol usually leaves the body quickly after the stress has finished but some of the girls still had raised levels days later. Sorry if this is all a bit too technical."

"So how do you interpret that?" asked one of the teachers.

"Well, it suggests that the stress is continuing."

"What sort of stress are we talking about?"

"Well, there's the question," said the doctor. "Physical, mental, toxic? At this moment, I have not much better idea than you do. And, to be perfectly honest, I am not quite sure how to progress. Except, that is, to seek advice from doctors who specialise in this area more than I do. I know a consultant at the Royal Free Hospital in London who has had a lot of dealings with epidemic disorders, that is conditions that affect a large group of people at once, and I know he has had some strange cases with which to deal. My suggestion is to ask him for his opinion."

With little alternative choice, the group agreed with his proposal but they could not be described as content. After the doctor had left, they gathered together in small huddles and talked things over. As alway occurs against a background of uncertainty, new ideas were volunteered freely.

"I still think it's that farmer, Arthur Black," said one. "He's always been a bit careless. Who knows what he's sprayed over the school? And I know you're going to say that all the tests for poisons were negative but maybe he's using a chemical that they haven't tested for."

"There have been a lot of funny goings-on in this area for quite a while now," said Margaret. "Do you remember we had those girls blacking out at the village fair all those years ago? That wasn't close to Arthur Black's fields; it was in the field of the old manor house."

"But no doubt they used chemicals on that field too from time to time," suggested one of the others.

Ignoring the counter-argument, she continued: "I just think there is some evil influence in our area. Even Arthur Black himself is losing his marbles."

"Oh come on, Margaret, lots of older people get confused and, in his case, the booze doesn't help!"

"What about the whole of last year? The wettest summer on record; a failed harvest; deaths of several bee colonies; an invasion of mosquitoes..."

"But they could all be connected!"

"That's what I am saying!"

"No, I mean, for example, simply the change in the weather might have caused all the other things to follow in its wake."

"Well, let's see what the next disaster is, shall we?" said Margaret, as most of her colleagues gave varying gestures of disapproval and began to turn away.

A week later, Dr. Soames was back in front of the group. They all waited in trepidation for the next announcement.

"I have now had an opportunity to discuss the case of the girls with Professor Swanson, who is the doctor I mentioned last time with experience in epidemic disorders, especially those which seem more bizarre or at least difficult to explain. I gave him all the details that you have so carefully documented about the nature and timing of the attacks and I showed him all the blood test results. I also showed him a map of the area, identifying the location of the school, the farmers' fields and any other geographical feature that could possibly be important."

"He agreed that poisoning from farm chemicals seemed very unlikely, given the negative blood test results and the fact that all the common farm chemicals in use in this country were tested for."

"He described to me a number of similar situations that have occurred in the past at a number of places throughout the world, including this country. In all cases, several people, sometimes very many, were afflicted with the same disorder over a short period of time. Not all these afflictions were blackouts; in fact, some of the disorders that affected people were extremely unusual but the common thread throughout all these different accounts is that everyone in a particular epidemic bout was affected in a similar way. That is to say, a bout of attacks in one place and at one time may be very different from a bout occurring somewhere else at a different time but, within each bout, all victims had more or less the same pattern of symptoms."

"Sorry, doctor," said one of the group, "but why is that so important?"

"Just what I was going to ask!" said another.

"Yes, I'm sorry," said Dr. Soames. "To give a proper explanation, it is difficult to avoid the detail and this background is important to what I will come to next. Imagine a disease - say something that you have caught from someone else. It may spread so a lot of people are affected at the same time but the symptoms will depend on the cause; the symptoms of bacterial food poisoning, for example, are quite different from those of measles. The bouts of attacks that have occurred over the years are all different so ought to have different causes - but no-one has managed to find a cause for any one of them, let alone all. The more causes there are, the greater the chance of identifying one of them. But it has not happened. That's a bit odd."

"What are these other attacks that have occurred over the years like and how long have they been going on?" asked the headmaster.

"Well, people have been reporting bouts of strange attacks over a long time, centuries in fact. In the sixteenth century, for example, something that has come to be called the dancing plague occurred in Strasbourg. Hundreds of people took to dancing in the streets quite involuntarily. It went on for several months, during which time many people died of exhaustion, heart attacks and so on."

"Dancing!" said one of the teachers. "But that's nothing like our girls - our girls were obviously ill!"

"And there was another, for example, that occurred more recently, in the 1940s, in America. It was a place called New Amboise. Lots of people believed they were being attacked by a mystery gasman - or woman - usually during the night. They woke up coughing and with eyes streaming and later became paralysed; some of them reported that they had smelt a strange odour around the time they developed the symptoms, which is why they initially thought they were being gassed. But again no poison could be identified. Fortunately, they all recovered. One interesting feature, by the way, is that virtually all the victims were young girls."

"Maybe we are getting too wrapped up in detail," said the headmaster. "Please, Dr. Soames, give us the bottom line, as they say."

"The bottom line is that no-one has ever found out what causes any of these attacks and maybe we have an opportunity to add to the research, if you and the girls are willing. There have been many theories. Going far back, the attacks were put down to witchcraft, an evil doing by some sorcerer within the community. But, of course, that was before we understood more about science and the working of the mind."

The teacher Margaret turned to her companion. "Now, what do you have to say?" she whispered. "I told you there were strange goings-on around here. And now we know: it's witchcraft!" Her companion ignored her and turned back to listen to the doctor.

"One current theory," continued Dr. Soames, "is that nobody can find a cause outside the body of those affected because the attacks all come from within, from a strange working of the mind. The strange working manifests itself in some unusual behaviour, whether that be dancing or blackouts, and then others witnessing the attack become affected because they are vulnerable and have a psychological reaction to what they have seen. This is all subconscious."

"With respect," said one of the group, "that sounds, to a lay person, very far-fetched. It also suggests that the girls are somehow mad, which, I can assure you, they are not."

"I can assure you too," said the doctor, "that I am in no way suggesting that any of the girls is mad. But, if the attacks have a psychological cause, people who are naturally anxious may be more vulnerable and chronic anxiety is one cause of persistently raised cortisol levels - the stress hormone. I am proposing that we give a series of psychological tests to the girls simply to measure the level of anxiety. The tests are really quite harmless."

The discussion continued in this vein for another fifteen to twenty minutes, by which time most of those with strong opinions had exhausted their inner prejudices and the more open-minded had bided their time, waiting for a forward plan of action. It was finally agreed that the girls and their parents would be approached to ascertain whether the girls would undertake further psychological tests to establish whether the attacks occurred preferentially amongst those with a particular personality type.

Two weeks later, the tests were completed amongst those girls who were willing to participate and Dr. Soames reported the findings to the group. He confirmed that a number of them had high levels of anxiety, which supported the theory that attacks occurred in those who were psychologically vulnerable.

"I have been thinking about what you said at our last meeting and just now," said the headmaster. "I am not a doctor but I cannot help wondering that the girls may now be persistently anxious not because they were like that before but because they remain frightened about the attacks that they and the other girls have had?"

The doctor paused. "Well, Mr. Cartwright, I have to admit that is a possibility."

Agreed that nothing more could be done at this stage, the meeting closed. As the group began to disperse, Margaret turned again to her colleague.

"Mark my words," she said, "as long as there are witches around, nobody will be able to rest in their beds."

Chapter 5

London UK August 1998

Jennie Black had only been in London for six days but already she was beginning to feel more calm. Understandably, perhaps, because in that short time she had managed to find herself an affordable, furnished flat and the kind lady at the employment agency where she registered was optimistic that Jennie would find a suitable job within a short period. Fortunately, the clerical market had recently opened up so there was a likely prospect there, which would be well within her abilities. It would also satisfy her wishes not to have too much public exposure. She would be able to move into the flat as soon as she had started work.

Her mind was unusually inactive as she travelled back on the tube to her temporary hotel so she hardly noticed the dark-haired man taking one of the few remaining available seats, next to hers. But, before long, she was jolted into awareness when the train lurched, they were both thrown forward and a major part of the contents of his plastic coffee cup landed on part of her beige skirt, over her left thigh. Normally, she would have been inclined not to worry unduly and to accept it as one of the hazards of travelling on a crowded London underground. But now the situation was different: she had limited funds, was not yet earning and the skirt was one of a few items of clothing that she had brought with her to London. It was obvious it would have to be taken in to be cleaned if she were to look at all respectable and she had nothing with which to replace it during its absence. Hence she was receptive, not only to his gushing apologies, but also to his offer to have the skirt cleaned and to buy her a replacement by way of compensation, just in case the cleaning was unable to restore the clothing to its original state.

This stranger turned out to be more interesting than she could have imagined from a random meeting on a tube train. He went far beyond his obligation and promise to pay for a replacement skirt and showed himself as quite a skilled opinion on matters of female appearance, as together they coursed around a series of select ladies' clothes shops, all chosen by him. No, he explained at one point, he was not a professional dress designer and he did not work in the industry but he did like to regard himself as observant and hoped he had good taste. She could not place his background; good taste he certainly had and he looked well groomed, almost handsome, but he did not seem overtly rich or upper class. *Just as well,* she thought; otherwise why would he have taken the trouble to bother about someone so obviously ordinary as she was? *Maybe he's just a nice guy.*

When she had chosen her skirt - and new blouse thrown in - he suggested, as she expected he would, that they go for coffee. She could hardly refuse after what he had done for her, despite its being his fault in the first place, but the reflex thoughts of many young women in this situation flooded her mind. *Is this the first step towards the inevitable payment for services rendered? After coffee, will he suggest that he take me to my hotel and escort me to my room or will it be a drink at his apartment? And then, refusal of his next request, if he bothers to ask, simply won't be on the cards.*

Was he a mind-reader too? With trepidation, she accepted the offer of coffee but, despite an urge to add a few qualifiers, then remained silent until he spoke: "And I mean just coffee," he said, looking into her eyes. "No, I am not going to suggest that you come back to my apartment or that I take you back to your hotel room afterwards." And then, after a pause, "Mind you, I can't promise that I won't ask you if you would be willing to see me again sometime." He smiled and she returned the gesture.

And so it started. By the end of their first day together, she had learned that he was called James and worked at a high street bank, hoping for promotion to manager within a few months, which might involve moving branch but he would remain in London. London was his birthplace and he had lived there all his life, mostly as a child with his parents in Cheam, but, since leaving home, in a variety of flats, some good, some not so.

He learned that she was called Charlotte - yes, Charlotte - and had moved from a life on a farm in the Cotswolds to find a more worldly life in the capital. He did not learn much more; in fact, she regretted telling him anything at all about herself because she knew that the main reason for escaping to London was to fade into obscurity and anonymity, hence the rapidly invented false name.

Within a few weeks, the two were spending virtually all of their spare time together. The question of common interests never really arose because they just relished each other's company and were happy whatever they were doing as long as they were together. Jennie found in James the raison d'être of the new life that she was seeking, made all the easier because he found no need to explore her past life; her presence with him in the here and now seemed sufficient. For her part, she had no desire to learn about his past life, partly because she did not want her enquiries to lead to a reciprocal demand from him about hers, but also because, like him, the beauty of the moment was enough for her. And every moment was a new moment which did not need the ones that had passed.

If either of them were required to explain what they found so attractive in the other, they would probably both have given similar responses, in the commonplace words of people in love: the chemistry, the magnetism, the sense of humour, the good looks, the "just getting on". But, like most lovers, their feelings for each other defied rational explanation because emotions like theirs are not conducive to an analysis by the method of language. Again like most lovers, they felt their relationship was unique.

As another symbol of the new-found life, James gave up his flat and moved with Jennie into the one that she had secured but which was new for both of them. Their one-bedroomed flat was on the third floor of a converted Victorian warehouse, not upmarket but not downtrodden either; it was "comfortable", as James reminded her often. It was not as large or as characterful as his but being forced to be closer together in a smaller space seemed only a good thing. The lift usually worked but, if not, she would tell herself that a brisk climb up the flights of stairs was welcome exercise after a day of immobility, which would maintain her muscles in some shape for the long weekend run around the park. It seemed that they had everything they needed; even their new cat seemed to sport a permanent smile.

Her love and admiration for James allowed him gradually to draw her out of her enforced reticence and solitude although she remained secretive about the details of her former life. But they did go out more than she had originally intended and, on her birthday, she could not resist his obvious desire to make the day a special one for her.

Jennie had always considered herself fortunate that her birthday fell on May 1st. Although sometimes at school on that day, the May Day bank holiday came soon afterwards. Combe Hollow always celebrated May Day in a traditional way with a village fete, including a maypole but, so that the children could join in, deferred the festivities to the bank holiday when the schools were closed. Jennie loved the dancing, the music, the laughter and especially when one year she was crowned May Queen. She did not notice that the crown was made of cardboard and her robes from a bedsheet; the sparkles on the tiara and the carefully painted bright colours on her gown were much more important. She knew she was a very important person and, not only that, she was able to keep her royal title until the celebrations the following year, a long time in the mind of an eight-year-old. Every year, her birthday seemed to extend continuously from the actual day to the May Day fete, much longer than that of any of her friends, who usually had only one day. When Jennie's birthday fell on a Saturday, it was even better because she did not have to go to school over the three days between her birthday and the May Day celebrations.

And so it was for her first birthday with James. Admittedly, no May Day celebrations but May 1st was a Saturday, when neither of them was working, and the weekend was all theirs. James had planned the Saturday: they would take the tube into central London, go boating on the Serpentine in Hyde Park and have lunch in Covent Garden. In the afternoon, they would visit one of the museums and take afternoon tea at the Ritz. He decided that they would not need dinner before they went to a

West End show but they could have a late supper with champagne at home on their return. Sunday should probably be a lazy day with a long walk, which they might well need after the day before.

No, he responded to her anxious questioning, they did not have a lot of money but they had enough and this was to be her special day, doing things that he guessed she had never done before. Anyway, he added, it was all settled because he had made the bookings - and paid for them. But, OK, he condescended, they would make the lunch a simple one.

Much to James' amazement, judging by the way she handled the boat when she took her turn, she did not fall in. He tried but failed not to laugh and her protests that she had never had to use a boat in the farmlands just provoked more laughter.

"It's a rowing boat! There are only two bits of apparatus you need worry about; they are called oars and you put one in each hand!"

"Thank you, James darling; I think I knew that."

He maintained that he had stuck to his promise that the lunch would be a simple one and it was his turn to protest when she pointed out that gravadlax salad accompanied by a glass of chilled chardonnay and followed by vanilla creme brûlée was not simple.

"You might know about boats but it looks like you don't know much about simple food!" she said, laughing.

"We eat simply all the time. This is just a little bit less simple."

"So it's all relative, I suppose."

"Exactly, my darling. Now you've got the idea."

146

After lunch, they wandered the London streets before heading for the British Museum. Jennie had not felt so free since her arrival in London and her worries about avoiding too much public exposure seemed to have dissipated, at least for the present. It was her birthday and she was having a wonderful time, full of fun and laughter, with the one she loved.

"Let's see what's going on in here," said James, as they walked up the approach to the neo-classical facade of the building.

"Wow, how many columns are there?" said Jennie.

"A lot, I'd say," said James.

Apart from the expense, Jennie felt no reason to resist when James suggested that they pay to visit the special exhibition on Witches Through the Ages and she knew that any objection on the grounds of cost would make little difference - and, in truth, she was pleased at the effort that James was making to give her a special day.

"I think it's mostly paintings," he said, examining the leaflet provided by the museum attendant. "Could be fun!"

They moved at a slow walking pace through the three rooms devoted to the exhibition, briefly studying every picture and scanning the text of the information boards placed at intervals around the walls. Neither of them was well versed in the world of art but both were taken by the powerful images in some of the pictures and the obvious skill of the artist who created them.

But one painting in particular caused Jennie to stop. A girl was seated at a wooden desk, writing; her face, her clothes and the desk were portrayed in bright colours, mostly shades of yellow. The area behind her was in much darker colours, dark browns and blacks, giving the impression that the writer was in a darkened room with her workspace illuminated by some invisible light. She was deep in concentration, focussing solely on her task and oblivious to her surroundings but standing behind her could be clearly seen the image of an older woman whose dark form seemed to merge with the background. This woman was doing nothing but staring at the back of the girl's head; her eyes were set and her face was expressionless.

Until now, Jennie had been impressed but also somewhat amused by the subjects of the pictures she had seen. Yes, they were dramatic but the images of people with hair of snakes and groups of women seated around a cauldron, entertained by a being with horns, a forked tail and carrying a three-pronged pitchfork were clearly from the world of fantasy. This picture was different for it seemed to represent something real although what that was she found hard to define. But two facets were made clear in the artist's representation: the girl was innocent and the woman was evil. And more: the woman was threatening. In an instant, she transfigured herself into the painting; this picture was a depiction of her life as it had become.

Jennie ran from the room and sat on one of the benches outside, her head bowed into her hands. James, seeing her suddenly flee, followed soon after, sat beside her and put his arm around her. Instinctively, she leaned her head onto his shoulder.

"What's wrong?" he asked.

"Nothing, nothing. I'm OK. Just one of the pictures made me a bit frightened. Sorry. I'm not usually like this."

He could feel her body trembling against his. "No, I know you're not. I feel like making a joke about those silly pictures - because that's what they are - but I can see you're really upset. You're not frightened of witches, are you? That doesn't sound like you. What was it? Was it something particular that reminded you of something?"

"No, really. It was just one of the pictures seemed somehow so horrible. I can't explain it. But maybe that's the effect that the artist wanted to produce. Honestly, I'm fine now."

Jennie sat quietly for several minutes nestled into James' chest and forced herself to regain her composure. Of course, in one sense, she wanted to tell James everything because he was the one person in the world with whom she could share her fears. But not this. No, she had to live it through alone. Maybe, one day, when she knew for sure that she was safe again, then she would tell him.

"Let's go for tea," she said, stood up and pulled him by the hand.

As she walked into the theatre to see the musical, Phantom of the Opera, for a moment the word "phantom" resonated through her brain but, by the time she had taken her seat, the drink in the bar had begun to take effect and she was now calmly determined to enjoy the show for what it was, a story with music. She was prepared to feel exhilarated and she did.

And yet, not always. Was it just her or was everybody affected the same way by the words as, with the accompanying music, they seemed to reverberate around the theatre from the front, sides and even behind? Yes, from behind. And there, in her mind, was the painting again.

Night time sharpens, heightens each sensation....Darkness stirs and wakes imagination....Silently the senses abandon their defences

Close your eyes and surrender to your darkest dreams....Purge your thoughts of the life you knew before....Close your eyes, let your spirit start to soar....In this darkness that you know you cannot fight

Let your mind start a journey through a strange new world....Leave all thoughts of the life you knew before....Let your soul take you where you long to be....Only then can you belong to me

Floating, falling sweet intoxication....Touch me, trust me, savour each sensation....Let the dream begin, let your darker side give in....To the power of the music that I write....The power of the music of the night

You alone can make my song take flight....Help me make the music of the night

Like her, James became pensive after that song but their motives were different.   A wonderful, thoughtful piece of musical writing, he thought; for Jennie, her mind was flooded again by a sense of persecution.   *Understandable maybe,* she thought, *but I've got to stop it, break my mind free and live my new life away from all that. That's why I came here; I've done it, found my love - yes, I've done it; this is where we begin!*

Despite being not far from a main road, the flat was quieter than expected, possibly because the noise was shielded from them by the other tall buildings around the periphery of their cul-de-sac.   However, the resulting tranquility and sense of isolation made the slightest extraneous noise all the more

150

noticeable. Thus it was that, one hour into retiring, Jennie was awoken one night by a noise that would in other situations not have disturbed her sleep. Certainly, it had not disturbed James as evidenced by his continuing snoring. Initially she lay motionless, some inner sense of dread rendering her semi-paralysed. Although still fearful of any untoward movement, she slowly half opened both eyes but saw nothing in the darkness.

But there was the noise: a rhythmic tapping noise, mixed with a high-pitched whine, that seemed to reach her from all the four walls of their bedroom. A mounting sense of concern for her safety and that of James prompted in her some feeling that something had to be done although she knew not what. And something about the noise led her to the firm belief that whatever she did would be futile. She forced herself to move. As she sat up in bed, the noise grew louder but James continued to sleep. It may have been her imagination, she thought at first, but it appeared that, within a few minutes, each noisy tap was accompanied by a bright flash of light across the ceiling. She sat transfixed, listening and watching in mounting anxiety. But she maintained enough self-awareness to realise that the increasing intensity of the noise and the lights may have been an exaggeration at least partly generated within her own mind. And she also knew that she was now predisposed to detect danger in every untoward experience.

She managed to maintain her composure as her perception of what she regarded as this Devil's son-et-lumière spectacle reached its crescendo: the heavy banging and wailing in quadrophonic sound and the dancing lights circling across the ceiling and walls and around her head. No longer was this anything to do with her imagination. When the bed began to vibrate, her tenacity broke.

"James, wake up!" she cried, shaking her partner vigorously. The intensity and tone of her voice and the violent movements of his body woke him abruptly.

"Charlotte, what on earth is the matter?"

"Something terrible is happening! Look at it - and listen to that!"

But, as soon as she had spoken, she realised that the room was once again dark and silent. No problems, no evidence, just her own protestations. He would be sympathetic, yes, but she knew that the display had been for her and her alone and its improbable nature meant that her account was unlikely to convince a rational man like James. So she underplayed it.

"I just heard some noises and saw some lights," she said, deliberately and purposefully calming herself.

He held her close to him for a couple of minutes, stroking her hair and ensuring that there was nothing tangible to create her distress. All remained dark and silent.

James turned on the bedside light. "Well, there's nothing now, my darling. You need fear no more. See - whatever it was has gone." He cupped her head in his hands and brought his face close to hers. In a whisper, he said, "Could it all have been a bad dream?"

She knew that it was not but she agreed that it probably was.

"Do you want to get up for a while? Can I get you a hot drink - or even something stronger? It might help to calm your mind and help you get back to sleep," he said.

"No, thank you, darling. I'm fine - I really am." She forced a smile.

"Try and go back to sleep," said James. He coaxed her back into a lying position, turned off the light and lay close to her with his arm wrapped around her waist, kissing her intermittently on the side of the head. Although still alert, she lay quiet, keen not to rearouse her partner and draw him into an alien world any more than she had done already. By ten to fifteen minutes later, his kisses had ceased, his arm had gone limp and his heavy breathing confirmed that she was again alone in her wakefulness. For the next hour and a half, she lay looking and listening but sensed only silence and darkness. Part of her felt that she dare not go back to sleep for it was in the sleeping state that the evil would return but, as her mind settled to the realisation that, whatever it was, it was not in her control, she drifted into unawareness.

"You had a really bad dream," said James the following morning, as he handed her the early morning cup of tea. "Are you ok now? I guess you got back to sleep again because you seemed pretty quiet afterwards. Well, at any rate, I didn't hear you!"

"Yes, thank you, darling. Just a silly old dream. I'm fine now."

Just a silly old dream. I don't think so, she thought.

Jennie Black arrived at her station fifteen to twenty minutes later than usual, the extra time in a crowded tube caused by the engineering works leaving her feeling particularly hot and dishevelled. Desperate for some fresh air, she moved as quickly as she could through the bustling rush-hour crowds and ran up the side of the elevator left free by those who were too weary to do more than stand.   She took several deep breaths as she passed through the station exit and slowed her pace for a gentle mind-settling fifteen-minute walk to her flat.

The plan for these normal weekday evenings was by now well established: James would arrive home from his work in about an hour, which allowed her time to readjust her mindset from a day in a tedious office, pour herself a glass of wine and start to generate some ideas as to what they might have for dinner. Then, unless James happened to be in one of his frisky

moods, they would, as usual, defer their plans of love-making and settle down in front of the television.

After opening the door that led into a small hallway opening directly into the kitchen, she threw her bag to the side behind the door. She flicked the switch that usually turned on the rack of four ceiling lights extending in a line across the kitchen ceiling from the hall to the far door into the sitting room. Only the light closest to her illuminated so, apart from a small area closest to the hall, the rest of the kitchen remained in semi-darkness.   Swearing under her breath at yet another failing of the home that she had always regarded as structurally inadequate, she flicked the light switch three or four more times before giving up in desperation and groping under the kitchen sink for a torch that they had bought when once they had suffered a two-day power cut.

With her head still buried in the cupboard, she suddenly became aware of a bright light behind her. Feeling a sense of relief that the fault had resolved spontaneously, she turned around and stood up. But the relief soon dissipated. Standing by the door was a middle-aged, gaunt woman dressed in a cheap, cotton dress, belted at the waist. Her hair was dark but greying. Her face was impassive; her eyes were staring, the effect magnified by the round rimless glasses. The light stemmed from a bright halo that seemed to surround her whole body.

Jennie screamed: "Leave me alone! Why are you plaguing me? What do you want?"

"I think you know what I want, Jennie - or Charlotte - or whatever name you now give yourself. I want you. They have harmed me beyond compare. Have you heard of an eye for an eye and a tooth for a tooth? Well, that is why I am here. Correct what they have done or the revenge will be sweet."

"I have done nothing!" screamed Jennie. "Tell me - what have I done?! What do you believe I have done? Or they - whoever they are - what have they done? And why are you torturing me for it?"

"They like to say that they deplore evil," sneered the woman, "yet they live their lives through their own form of evil - deceit, lying, manipulation, getting their own way for their own gains and blaming innocent people, even children, for things they have brought upon themselves. And they push their sanctimonious, distorted ideas regardless of who else may suffer. Well, now everyone else will suffer unless amends are made - by you, in particular. I have chosen you because you have the chance to appease the wrongdoings of all the others and giving me back what is mine. I told you - an eye for an eye and a tooth for a tooth. And that carries on until what is mine is returned to me."

"What have I done?" shouted Jennie again, tears flooding down her cheeks and sweat dripping from her temples. "Please tell me - what have I done?"

"You may have done nothing but those others know very well what they have done. Fix it now before it is all too late."

The light dimmed but the woman was still clearly visible. As she stopped speaking, the floor began to shake. Eventually, Jennie could maintain her balance no longer and fell to the floor. As she looked upwards, she saw that the woman had approached more closely and seemed to have increased in size such that she was now towering over her.

"Do you understand?" said the woman. There followed a silent pause of several seconds that seemed to Jennie like hours when her pet cat, Manxie, suddenly ran into the kitchen from one of the neighbouring rooms. It ran close to Jennie who had just enough time to gain brief comfort from holding it close before it went suddenly stiff, stopped breathing and collapsed immobile by her side.

"Understand?" said the woman. Then, as if from nowhere, she produced a framed photograph of James that Jennie kept by her bedside, her first vision of her loved one on waking in the morning, until she turned over to be in his arms. The whole frame and photograph broke into tiny fragments in the woman's hand and fell to the floor.

"Understand?" she said again.

Jennie screamed in terror, closed her eyes and placed both hands over the top of her head, with her forearms pressed down over both ears. For maybe just a moment - a moment for which she would be thankful - that and her loud sobbing seemed to cut out the voice of the woman and the noise of any other disasters that she might choose to invoke around her. Jennie felt barely able to move and prayed that she could just stay in that state of isolation for ever but eventually - she did not know how much time later but it seemed like hours - she stopped crying, lifted her forearms slightly and listened. Silence. Gradually, she eased her hands from her head and opened her eyes. *Thank God, she has gone!*

Jennie turned over onto her back and looked around her. The one light that had turned on when she arrived home remained lit and the kitchen was just as it always was. Suddenly, she became aware of a shuffling noise coming from the bedroom; her heart began to race again and she began to breathe heavily but, just as she started to prepare herself for the next ordeal, she collapsed back to the ground in relief as Manxie ran out of the bedroom door towards her and nestled his head under her chin. Holding him close to her, she kissed him furiously around his neck and then jumped up to standing to look for the fragments of the broken photograph. Nothing. She ran into the bedroom and stopped abruptly, gasping in amazement. On the bedside table, as usual, was the framed photograph of James, undamaged.

So now a second time. But did she need to be reminded of the horrors that might be inflicted upon her? She could hardly forget; it was made clear enough the first time.

Jennie had come over to the farm to see her father as she did every weekend since she moved out of the house. In many ways, she regretted having left him because he was becoming increasingly frail and, if anything, needed her more than ever. So, on this occasion, with a particularly strong feeling of guilt, she had decided to stay for the Friday and Saturday nights. Over breakfast on the Saturday morning, everything seemed so normal again, her father sitting opposite munching rather indelicately into his cornflakes and slurping intermittently from his mug of coffee and her liberally spreading her home-made marmalade over the two pieces of toast. He did not speak as much as he used to do but he still managed to recount some of his now familiar stories about how difficult farming was for his parents in the years after the war and even by the 1960s, when he was a very young man, Britain was importing most of its beef from abroad. Times were particularly hard in their small rural community, which is why he and Jennie's mother had to wait before deciding they had enough money to bring a child into the world. But, as he always added, the wait was worth it because they were then blessed with a wonderful daughter.

So did she really have to leave? Well, maybe not but she reminded herself that the main reason was for the sake of her father. She did not know why Megan had changed but changed she had. So kind, friendly and attentive to the whole family at first, that all changed, especially after her mother disappeared. She visited more and more often until eventually it seemed that she hardly left the house. Jennie knew that, even as she sat with her father at breakfast that weekend of her visit, it would not be long before Megan appeared. But it was not just excessive visits; those in themselves could be welcome. No, it was the way that she treated Jennie that made her increasingly uncomfortable. Control, demands, almost possession, to the extent that, in the end, Jennie did not feel that she could do anything without Megan's approval or go anywhere far from her side. Maybe she could have handled the personal distress but it was the effect it was having on her father that she found hard to bear. It was obvious that he was becoming increasingly isolated and separated from his daughter, emotionally if not physically, and his discomfort showed. And the father's discomfort became the daughter's discomfort.

Jennie convinced herself that, if she were not a permanent resident of the house, she could loosen the bonds between her and Megan and the relationship with her father might revert more to how it used to be, on the occasions that she visited. Her father would not have to suffer the constant strains forced on to the relationship with his daughter and might gain positive benefit from Megan's presence if Jennie were not around. Indeed, she had noticed that, on the increasingly few occasions that she had managed to distance herself from her attentions, Megan's care for Jennie's father seemed much richer.

And, yes, later that Saturday morning on Jennie's weekend stay at the farmhouse, Megan did arrive and, yes, her behaviour was much the same. But, at least, she left around six o'clock, leaving Jennie and her father to break into aperitifs, him one of his favourite beers and her the first of several glasses from a bottle of her favourite chardonnay that she brought with her.

Her sense of being back home was reinforced as she walked into her familiar bedroom and settled beneath the sheets in her familiar bed. This was the bed that she had slept in since the earliest childhood she could remember, at first with her cuddly velvet rabbit and later her Barbie doll. As she settled her head against the pillows, the memories of her childhood cascaded through increasing drowsiness until she settled into deep sleep.

She believed that she was woken by natural bodily function, a desire to visit the loo. So she was sure that she was conscious on returning from the bathroom and the experience she had was real and not a dream. It was a person, without doubt, but it had an abstract form, standing immobile at the far side of her bed. It did not need to speak to impart fear for somehow that was implicit in its being but speak it did.

"Hello Jennie." Jennie was transfixed and did not speak. She stared in horror, disbelief and incomprehension.

"Hello Jennie. The time has come for you to leave this world, for you to start a new life with me, a life as my daughter."

Jennie fell onto the bed and covered her eyes but the image remained visible. She covered her ears but the voice was just as audible. The repetitive barracking continued for maybe five or ten minutes but it seemed like hours. Although to Jennie what the voice said made little sense, nevertheless every word seemed to cut deep into her soul; every word made her body tremble with terror. When finally the image and voice disappeared, the fact that Jennie could not explain what had happened made little difference to the lasting sense of persecution and overwhelming vulnerability that now seemed an integral part of her whole being. Although it had never been said, something made it obvious that this thing, whatever it was, would return. And Jennie had to get away.

And now, here in London, far enough, she thought, to hide away and escape, the creature had found her again. It may not have looked exactly as it did when it appeared to her in Combe Hollow, but the essence of its nature was unmistakably the same.

Jennie knew that now she had to leave London, to melt into obscurity somewhere that this being, whatever it was, could not find her. Yes, she had tried once already but clearly not well

160

enough.   She had not completely hidden away and she had made the mistake of falling in love, thereby risking not only herself but also someone who had no place in this saga, whatever it was, and for whom she cared deeply. She could risk no more; she could not risk her only love, James; she had to leave for somewhere.   Hastily, she packed the minimal of belongings. She wrote a quick note to James to say that she had to deal urgently with something from the past and would be away for the night. He knew that her past was rather secretive and had got used to it so she hoped he would not be too surprised or distressed at her sudden absence for a short while. She vowed she would post him a proper letter when she had settled her mind; she hardly knew what she could say because, however she phrased it, his reaction to the news that she had gone for ever would be something quite different, that she knew. But she also knew that she had no choice; the alternative was unthinkable. She left the flat.

Chapter 6

London UK May 1999

Julian was deep in the newspaper archives. Not much more to add than he could remember, he thought, not surprisingly because the case had impacted so much upon his mind at the time. Except one thing that he had forgotten: Charlotte had disappeared suddenly from her home in Hackney *where she had been resident for only a few months.* So where had she come from and why? Had she simply moved flat within London, possibly to be with her boyfriend? Had she come from outside the city in the seeking of adventure by a young girl? Or could it just be that, given her sudden exit from Hackney, she had fled there to escape from somewhere else? And, if so, why? Or is this all the overactive imagination of a journalist? And what exactly did the police know about her background? Well, he would not let it rest. He had to visit Hackney and probably also speak to the police, who might have their interest rekindled by the letter he had found. Except that, so far, he could not prove that the author of the letter and the missing girl in his newspaper articles were one and the same. No, he would visit Hackney first and speak to the police later.

A few minutes from the station, Julian studied the map and his notes one more time. Burlington Court - cannot be more than ten to fifteen minutes' walk from the station. He looked once more from the window; it seemed like a fairly normal London suburb with a busy main road going through the centre that seemed to be not far from her presumed home.

He walked out of the station and stopped for a few moments just outside the exit. Looking down the main road, he reflected on how many times the missing girl, Charlotte, had trodden the route before him. Did she work out of the area and, at the end of each day, arrive like him at this point? Or perhaps she worked locally, in one of the shops, bars or restaurants. No doubt he would find out in due course.

Julian ambled down the main street, taking in the places that Charlotte may have visited on her way home from the station - a dry cleaners, a pet shop, a couple of banks and some coffee shops - and that he would come back to visit later. Turning off the main road and following the side streets, he arrived at a large, imposing, redbrick Victorian building that, once knowing better days, now looked rather tired. The facade was in need of a good clean and the windows no longer had the gleam of the originals. After confirming from the grey plaque at the side of the large, wooden entrance door that this was indeed Burlington Court, he stepped back a few paces to ponder what purpose the building had before being converted into middle-grade flats. *A warehouse, perhaps - or possibly some administrative building? No, probably a warehouse.* But that did not matter now because, fairly certainly, this was the place that Charlotte fled from. Julian was glad that he had located her residence but was not surprised that, in itself, it gave no clues to the reason for her disappearance: a refurbished building in one of the smaller streets of a typical London borough; nothing more than that. It was also clear that no information would be forthcoming from her neighbours in the other flats; there was no public entrance or call buttons and somehow the building seemed to be stating that it was either currently deserted or its residents had gone into hiding.

No, as he suspected, the information, at least for today, would have to come from elsewhere. He returned to the main street. His hunch that she might often have popped into a local food shop on her way home proved correct at his first point of enquiry, a mini-supermarket at the end of her cul-de-sac.

"Yes, I remember the missing girl very well," said the man behind the till. "This is my shop so I spend most of my time here. I get to know the locals quite well because they often call in for something to eat or drink on their way to work - people these days don't seem to have time for breakfast at home - or they might pick up some food for dinner on their way back - often accompanied by a bottle of wine - depending how their day has been, I guess! Charlotte she was called, I believe."

"Yes indeed. Thank you," said Julian. "What did you know about her?"

The man's reticence in talking about someone else, particularly a young girl who was now missing, was eased gradually as Julian explained the purpose of his visit and his professional involvement in the case since its beginning. Eventually, it seemed as if the man was keen to talk, having had no previous opportunity to share his thoughts.

"She seemed to be a lovely girl. In fact, they were a lovely couple - she had a boyfriend and they obviously adored each other. So sad - they had only been here a few months before she disappeared and then, of course, so did he in such a tragic way. The police suspected that he had killed her but anyone who knew them both would know that was impossible; he thought far too much about her."

"No, I don't know where she came from; in fact, nobody seemed to. Although she was very friendly and sociable, at least whenever I saw her, she kept her personal life very much to herself. Sadly, you know what gossips are - a certain number of people couldn't stop speculating about her background and you would sometimes see a small group of the worst offenders huddled together at one end of the shop while she was getting on with her business at the other. I tried to keep out of it but, as a shopkeeper, it was sometimes difficult. There was a rumour around for a while that she had moved from a farm in the country, near Cheltenham, I think. I don't know whether that was pure guesswork on the part of the gossip-mongers or whether she had let it slip in one of her unguarded moments - maybe under the constant interrogation of the nosey-parkers. I don't know."

"Do you know why she might have moved from the farm?" said Julian.

"No," said the proprietor. "As I said, I don't even know if it is true. The dreamers could no doubt concoct a story for you!"

As it turned out, that first visit of Julian's day turned out to be the most productive. Or so he thought. Yes, he had only got one piece of speculative information, about where she had come from, but it was a lead - a good one by the standards of most journalist's leads - and no-one else that day could add anything more. Everyone he spoke to, however, was agreed that she was a charming girl who would not harm anyone, that she was in a loving relationship and it was all very tragic.

He wandered the streets of Hackney in thought for a while until some impulse took him back to Burlington Court.

Number 9, he thought, as he stared again at the building. *Which one would that be?* He scanned the ground floor and first floor windows, four on the lower tier and four on the upper. And then the third floor. *Probably numbered from left to right so 9 is up there on the left.* Studiously, he examined the window of the girl's presumed flat but all that came to mind was her sitting there, overlooking the street. *What would she be thinking? What would she be doing?* As he continued to look, it began to rain heavily. He moved to the other side of the street under the shelter of a doorway's arch. The rain poured down the front of the building in rivulets through the irregular brickwork, taking bits of dust and grime in its path. Was it pure imagination that next attracted his attention? The course of the water over the structure and windows of flat number 9 was like tears streaming down full cheeks.

Julian had never thought of himself as the obsessive type - conscientious and a pursuer of the truth, yes, but not someone prone to fixation on a problem for which there would never be an answer. After all, his working life depended on results, the generation of newspaper stories. Some, he would concede, were based on less true fact than others - why ruin a good story with the facts, as someone once said - but he had always known when to give up and to pursue something else. So why was this girl, just another missing girl, demanding so much of his time and attention? He did not know but something was driving him on to continue the quest: some sense of honesty, some sense of fairness, some sense of respect and love of people.

His day in Hackney was good, he kept convincing himself. He had seen where she used to live and found that she probably came from a farm somewhere near Cheltenham. But, of course, in truth it was not enough. His time was running out on that day and he had to return home. *I'll just have to come back.*

As he prepared to walk back to the railway station, he made one last call to the supermarket that he had first visited, not this time to glean information but much more simply to buy a packet of crisps and a bottle of fruit juice to consume on the train back. However, he was rewarded with more than sustenance.

"Hello again!" said the proprietor, as Julian entered the shop.

"It's ok," said Julian, "I'm not hear to grill you any more. I just need a snack for the train." He started to move towards the shelves, when he was interrupted.

"Well, funnily enough," said the proprietor, "but one of the people who may be able to help you is over there, near the cereal packets," and then, lowering his voice to a near whisper, "but I'd be careful what you believe." He smiled.

The rather short, stocky lady of about mid-forties was scrutinising each cereal packet in detail, seeming to compare the ingredients of each, but she was more than happy to give up the task to share her knowledge and experience with Julian. She returned her glasses to their case, looked him in the face and smiled. It did not take long before he was able to get to the crucial questions.

"Yes, she came to live here from a farm in a village called Combe Hollow a few miles from Cirencester, Gloucestershire. She lived there with her father. Well, to be honest, I'm not sure if she actually lived on the farm or just nearby but it was obviously part of her life. How do I know, did you say? Well, because she told me!" She gave a broad grin of self-satisfaction, obviously pleased with the knowledge that she had a rare talent to extract information from people.

"Why do you think she would tell you, if you don't mind my asking," said Julian, "because apparently she was reluctant to talk about her past life to anyone?"

"Well, for a start I am a good listener," said the woman with another smile, "but I think I caught her in a bad moment. I met her in the park where she was sitting alone just staring into space. I sat on the bench next to her and just started to talk. I thought it might help. I think something had happened that had upset her. She didn't tell me anything about it - or about herself really - but, at one point, she told me that she had come to this area from Combe Hollow in the country, where her father had a farm. I think she told me that because she said that all she wanted was peace and that is why she had come here. But I guess she hadn't found it, for some reason."

"No, I don't know exactly why she left her previous home," she said in response to further questioning. "It wasn't to be with her boyfriend, though, I can tell you that, because she met him in London after her arrival here. I always got the impression that she was a bit frightened. I definitely saw it on that day in the park but I think it was there at other times too. Most people couldn't see it but I could. Maybe she was trying to get away from something."

Julian decided to press further. "And why do you think she left Hackney, so suddenly it seems?"

"Ah, well there's the million-dollar question that everybody has been asking since she left! And, of course, nobody knows for sure. But you are right, she certainly left in a hurry. It couldn't have been to get away from James - that's her boyfriend

- sorry, that was her boyfriend - because they adored each other. Well, in my opinion, they did and, if you don't mind me saying so, I'm a pretty good judge of people and I'm a pretty good observer too."

"Do you make it your business to be? Sorry, I didn't mean that unkindly but it sounds as if you are someone who is interested in people."

"Yes, I think that's fair. But, of course, I never intrude."

"No, of course not." He paused, then continued: "So, sorry to press you, but, from what you have seen, can you think of any reason at all why she might have left in such a hurry?"

The woman stretched herself upright and folded her arms across her chest. She took a deep breath, held it for a few moments and then exhaled deeply. *Here it comes*, thought Julian.

"She was frightened, very frightened. She came here to escape from something but obviously felt she had gained no peace. Even James could not give her the calm that she sought. In fact, if you think about it, it is obvious - she loved him and he loved her; the last thing she wanted to do was to leave him but leave him she had to do. And only something awful could have led her to do that. She would have known the distress it would have caused him, proven, I might say, by the tragic end that happened to him. But still something made her do it. And that has to be something terrible, something that frightened her beyond belief."

Is this the fantasy of a woman with a more than average imagination or could she be speaking some sense? She had paused in her speech but Julian resisted the temptation to interrupt. He kept silent.

"Maybe it was the same thing that caused her to come here in the first place," she added with a knowing look.

Maybe - or maybe not, thought Julian. How much could he believe this woman, especially given the scepticism of the shopkeeper, who knew her far better than he did? But that was all he had to go on - and he had to pursue it. To piece the whole story together, Julian needed to establish why she had left her previous home and then why she had left Hackney and where she had gone to. *First things first. Looks like the next stop will be Combe Hollow.*

"Thank you." He went to the station.

Julian stopped his car in the lay-by as he saw Combe Hollow village coming into sight down in the valley, got out and stood on the verge. The scene from the vantage of the hilltop was, to his eyes, a typical English pastoral scene, intensified by the bright sun that created bold contrasts amongst the colours of the buildings, land and water. Lines of perfectly aligned terraced stone cottages bordered the small river that flowed gently yet briskly through the village whilst more randomly placed small stone cottages stood in second, third and fourth tiers up the hillside behind them. Around the periphery of the buildings were vast areas of farmland, broken up into large but manageable fields by hedgerows that gave an air of permanence, stability and belonging. *For how many years, decades, centuries has that scene remained unchanged, save for the occasional development superimposed in the name of progress?* he thought. As he cast his eyes around the land, he spotted a more modern, yet still old, building between the edge of the village and one of the fields with an old clock tower and a more closely cut area of grassland adjacent to the building. Several cars were parked nearby. *Looks like a school.* Within the large field itself, at the edge nearest the school, was a ramshackle collection of farm buildings, in the centre of which was an old farmhouse.

Julian, who at least in recent years had spent much of his life in the claustrophobia of London's streets, offices and underground trains, viewed the scene before him as an idyll of peace and scarcely one from which someone would want to escape, particularly in some kind of fear. His mind was tending to reject the interpretation of events offered by the lady in the London supermarket in favour of his original hypothesis, a rural girl seeking a bit of adventure in London. But he knew he must investigate. He returned to his car.

He parked on the road beside the river, walked onto the centre of the old stone bridge and looked again at this quintessential English rural scene at closer hand. How many artists over the centuries must have sat in this spot and painted the image before him? He could practically still see, at least in his mind's eye, the workers in their seventeenth-century costumes carrying the wool from their honey-coloured stone weavers' cottages the short distance to the river to be washed. *But, in truth, maybe we guard an over-romanticised view of life back then,* he thought; *maybe it wasn't so peaceful here then - and maybe it isn't now.*

Where was he to start? Well, the only piece of evidence he had so far, and indeed the one that had led him to this village, was that the girl came from a farm - and, as far as he could see, there was fortunately only one in the village. He set off in the direction of the farm he had located from the hilltop.

Why do all farms look the same - and all so disorganised? he thought, as he passed the discarded, broken machinery and vats of chemicals in the yard before reaching the front door of the farmhouse. He waited for a few minutes after his third bout of vigorous knocking and was just about to abandon his efforts when the door was opened by a middle-aged woman with grey hair, round glasses and an impassive expression. She stared at him but said nothing.

"I am so sorry to disturb you," he began, "but I was hoping to have a few words with the farmer." Avoiding his impulse to stereotype her as the typical farmer's wife and not the key mover in the farm, he continued: "Would that be you?"

"No, it would not," she replied blandly, "and the farmer is not here. And he won't be back again either so there is no point in coming back." Before he was able to muster up the charm that many years in journalism had taught him as the key to extracting information from reluctant witnesses, particularly, dare he suggest it even to himself, women, the door was closed in his face. He made a feeble attempt to recruit her cooperation by knocking again but he sensed it was fruitless and left.

As he retraced his steps to the centre of the village, he took a detour to examine in more detail what he took to be the school. A school it obviously was and he had little doubt that the teachers there would know something about a girl who had left the village and probably the whereabouts of the proprietor of the adjacent farm. However, he deduced that he had arrived at lesson time and to disturb them then seemed inappropriate so he decided to seek his information elsewhere, initially at least. He could always return later.

As he passed over the stone bridge, instead of turning right back to his car, he took a left turn and walked along the road on the bank of the river. Within a couple of hundred yards, he came across a small hotel, again built of stone, with small paned windows and clad over its front face with Virginia creeper. A multi-faceted, iron lamp hung by the wooden entrance door; in the centre of a stone-flagged front terrace was a pond and fountain. *An old coaching inn, I presume, now the escape of tourists seeking a break in the country. Probably a good place for gossip.*

He was pleased to find that the receptionist was a girl, probably in her early twenties; he knew from experience that she would probably be more forthcoming than someone who, in later life, had learned to be more discrete. It did not take him long to gain her confidence and he suspected that she was secretly rather pleased to be talking to an investigative journalist; maybe this was the most exciting thing that had happened to her in some time.

"Oh, yes," said Julie with a broad smile, "I know the family well. I've lived in the village all my life so I know almost everybody, As for Mr. Black - the farmer, that is - he sadly died several months ago, maybe longer. It was no surprise, according to my mum at least, because apparently he had not been well for a long time."

"No, I don't really know," she said in response to further questions, "but I believe he had some sort of memory problem. I don't think he was coping very well. You certainly didn't see him around as much as you used to do."

"The girl that left? Jennie? That was his daughter. Yes, she did live with him but she left the family home not long after her mother died - or disappeared, should I say. That was a bit of a surprise but she was very close to her mother, much more than her father, in fact, so maybe it was the shock and that she couldn't cope with being at home without her mother in the same house. But she did continue to visit him at weekends. Then she left the area not long before Mr. Black died. Quite suddenly actually so that was even more of a surprise to everyone, especially since her father was obviously not well at the time and she didn't tell anyone where she was going."

In those few sentences, the girl had told Julian a lot but virtually every fact she conveyed was, to him, clouded in confusion.

"Did you say she was called Jennie?"

"Yes, Jennie Black. Jennifer, I suppose, but she was always known as Jennie."

"Was she also known as Charlotte?"

"No, definitely not. She was about my age so we practically grew up together. I have never heard her called that."

"Do you have any idea at all why she left? From what you say, you must have known her well and been fairly close to her."

"Yes, I would call her a friend - not a very close one, you understand, because she lived her own life and I lived mine - but we met at social things from time to time and have even been out together on occasions. No, I don't know why she left. I don't think anyone does really. We all assume that it was the continuing shock of her mother dying and she just wanted to get away and start a new life somewhere else."

"Do you think that you were sufficiently close to her that she would have likely told you why she was going, if she was going to tell anyone?"

"Well, I would like to think so, yes, but, if she left in a big hurry, maybe she didn't get the chance."

"She wouldn't have made a special effort to tell you if you happened not to be around?"

"No. probably not. I don't think we were quite that close."

Is this really the same girl that I am looking for? he thought. *It must be - I was told that Charlotte came from here and had a father with a farm. I find out that a girl did leave in a hurry and it would probably be about the time that she arrived in London. But the name is different. I have to believe it's the same girl. So the only realistic interpretation is that she changed her name when she got to London. And she left in a hurry. With no forwarding address. She must have been running away from something - or in a very disturbed state of mind, maybe, as the girl said, caused by the distress from her mother's disappearance. Or both. And maybe that woman in the shop who I thought might be fantasising is right after all.*

After he had wound down the conversation by shifting the topic to more mundane subjects, he expressed his profuse thanks to the young lady, promised to keep her informed and was about to leave when he stopped.

"Just one more thing, Julie: I called at the farm and was greeted - well, maybe that's overstating the case - was met by a middle-aged woman at the door. Do you know who that is?"

"Yes," said Julie, "that's Megan. She befriended Jennie and then got to know her parents. She spent a lot of time at the house, I guess because she was close to Jennie - Megan didn't really get on with her mother. She stayed on at the farm after Jennie left and looked after her dad in his later months. She's looking after the farm now until something can be sorted out."

"Why did she not get on with her mother?"

"Oh, I don't know really. Jennie's mother was very protective. Maybe Megan was jealous or something. I don't know; I'm just guessing."

"Megan seemed a bit abrupt. Is she ok?"

"Oh yes, she's fine. That's just her manner. She was very kind to Mr. Black when he was alive."

"Thank you again, Julie. Most grateful. No doubt see you again. Goodbye for now."

It was now past four o'clock and Julian calculated that soon the children would have left the school but the teachers would still be available. A good time to see what he could pick up from them, he decided. But first he took a detour behind the hotel to get a better idea of the village and its layout; he had been in the business long enough to know that sometimes clues can come from the most unexpected quarters and it was better to leave no stone unturned.

The streets were as expected from what he had seen already: narrow, irregular routes through strings of cottages with, apart from their occupants and some gestures towards modernity, probably little change over two hundred years or more. A few, which originally must have been dwellings, had now been converted to shops but it seemed the village had been able completely to resist the high street chains; no doubt the geographical layout would not have been conducive to the kind of new building that those brands would demand either. Half-way down one street that ascended gently up the first part of the hillside was the post office - *a statutory requirement in a village like this*, thought Julian, *and a great find for me because, after all, postmasters and mistresses know everything that's going on, do they not?*

The ruddy faced, rotund, jovial lady behind the counter confirmed that she was indeed the postmistress, that she had lived in the village all her life, had seen a lot of comings and goings and didn't believe that she had ever had a need to speak to a man from the newspapers before. The last statement seemed particularly amusing to her because it was followed by a long, hearty laugh - the sort of laugh that betrays some innnermost thoughts that its generator is unwilling to share. But fortunately her reticence did not extend to the world at large because soon she showed herself as a willing communicator. Unfortunately, however, she did not have much to add to what the girl in the hotel had told him. Except one thing.

Beryl - "call me Beryl" - was not quite as trusting as the hotel receptionist. No, she explained, she did not have quite such a rosy view of Megan. In her job, dealing with people, she had learnt quite a bit about human nature. No doubt there are some who are totally self-sacrificing but more often their kindness is a front for an underlying desire to gain something for themselves.

"I didn't see much of Megan, I have to say, because she kept herself to herself - apart from with the Black family, that is - but I probably saw more of her than most people because she came in here from time to time to post things or pick up parcels, mostly for the family in fact. Anyway, I think I saw enough of her and spoke to her enough to get a decent impression."

"And what was that?"

"Well, there was something about her I didn't like. It's hard to put a finger on it but I thought she seemed to be after something, I don't know what. But she seemed to be a bit of a control freak and why would she spend so much time with the Blacks?"

"Some people have said that she seemed to be a caring sort of person and that she was particularly friendly with Charlotte - sorry, Jennie," said Julian. "Obviously, that's not your impression but why do you think they would come to that conclusion?"

"Well, of course I have no real idea but I will say I find it hard to understand why a middle-aged woman would want to befriend a young girl. I suspect that her caring nature was a front and that really she was a bit manipulative, probably using Jennie for some other purpose - as I said, to get something for herself. Maybe I shouldn't have these thoughts but I have wondered if she was trying to get her hands on the farm, especially knowing that Arthur was not well and particularly after his wife died."

"But surely he would leave it to his daughter."

"Yes - but then again she became even more involved with Arthur after Jennie disappeared. Just suppose, God forbid, that Jennie was never found. Then Arthur dies and Megan claims that she was his partner and had a claim to his estate. I've heard of similar things happening in the past."

"Indeed," said Julian.

As is often the case when people pour out their opinions to a stranger, Beryl then rapidly backtracked on everything she had said, explaining that it was, of course, only her opinion - an impression - and she would not want to besmirch anybody unjustly. She had no real evidence for the things she had said and others may well think differently. Perhaps she had spoken out of turn; she was only trying to help. And the most important thing was to find Jennie; that was all she really cared about. A lovely girl.

Well, no evidence is probably right, thought Julian, *but sometimes people are very good at judging other people's characters.* He had learnt a long time ago not to disregard anything he had been told.

Julian returned to the school, judging his time between when the pupils would all have left and the headmaster was probably still in his office, finishing the day's work before he too returned home. *Strange, isn't it*, he thought after five minutes' conversation with John Cartwright across his desk, *how people's manner differs so much according to their roles? The hotel receptionist, the postmistress and now the headmaster are all different; I wonder which came first, the personality choosing the job or the job dictating the personality?* The headmaster was willing to help but he was naturally reserved and cautious, unwilling to say anything for which there was no evidence or authoritative back-up and using short sentences that were to the point. At least, at first.

It appeared that Mr. Cartwright had no clear idea, any more than anybody else, why Jennie had suddenly left the village and indeed the only untoward thing that had happened in recent times was the unexplained illness that had affected many girls in his school the previous year. Yes, he confirmed that those attacks had taken place but he could not provide details of the cases for reasons of confidentiality. In any case, nobody had suggested a link between those attacks and Jennie's disappearance and, apart from the close time relationship - she left maybe a couple of months after the attacks - he could not propose one.

But, after fifteen to twenty minutes of rather stilted conversation, John Cartwright suddenly relaxed. Placing both hands flat on the desk, he bent forward and began speaking freely directly towards Julian. The girls' attacks, and not the disappearance of Jennie Black, were clearly those which occupied him most. He was very worried, he explained, about the blight that had affected his school, not only for the welfare of the girls, which was, of course, his primary concern but also for the reputation of the school itself. Dr. Soames, the specialist investigating, he clarified, had offered the explanation that a case of mass hysteria may have occurred, spreading symptoms from girl to girl by some kind of psychological mechanism. It would not be unreasonable, the headmaster suggested, for any concerned parent to wonder why such a phenomenon had occurred and, moreover, what influence the school had had in generating the disturbed thought processes that were presumed to underlie it. Theirs was an independent school, he continued, which relied on a good reputation and parental support to continue to attract students. Without an adequate number of talented applicants, the income of the school would fall and it would become financially unstable. "In fact," he stated, "the number of applicants has fallen off over the last year, despite the attacks apparently having ceased. Presumably people are afraid that they may come back; the staff certainly are. I know that this is not the main reason for your coming to see me but it is something very unusual to occur in our village."

"Naturally," he said, drawing himself back for a moment, "I am voicing these concerns in complete confidence. To be honest, I probably should not be doing so at all especially, dare I suggest, to a member of the press but I admit to being extremely anxious about it all and I am afraid you are the one who has become the target for expression of those anxieties. I am sorry." He went quiet.

"Mr Cartwright," said Julian, adopting a tone of genuine sincerity, "I am a journalist but I am not here primarily in that capacity. I am here because I am concerned for the welfare of a girl who went missing from a flat in Hackney, London a few months ago. Yes, I was first involved when I reported the story for my newspaper but the interest in the case has now extended far beyond that. I want to know what has happened to her. The whole business is becoming more mysterious by the minute and everything that you can tell me, however irrelevant it seems, may help. I am also, as I hope a caring human being, concerned for you, the girls and your school. Anything I can offer, not as an expert, but as someone who, in their professional life, has come across a lot of strange things, I would gladly do. I can assure you that our conversation will remain entirely confidential."

The headmaster smiled and resumed his relaxed air. A journalist, yes, but what he said sounded genuine. And John had to speak to someone. He knew that none of his staff could fulfil the role; they were too wound up in their own concerns and expected him to exercise control; any sign of weakness would further undermine the functioning of the school. And his wife already thought that he devoted too much mental energy to his job.

"Apparently, this is not the first time this sort of thing has happened," said the headmaster, breathing deeply. "Not here, I mean, but in many other places throughout the world over a long period of time. They are not the same as has happened to my girls - well, actually some are almost identical - but most take a different form. Dr. Soames, the public health specialist, mentioned something that happened in America, in a place called New Amboise, which according to the latest expert opinion was also an example of mass hysteria. His comments prompted me to do some research of my own. Over the last few months, I have spent a lot of time seeking out and examining reports from a wide variety of sources about the case that he mentioned and others besides."

"And what did you find?"

"There have been many similar episodes and what I understand from what I have read is that, in all cases, no satisfactory explanation has been discovered. For example, in Canada at the end of the nineteenth century, sixty students at a ladies' seminary had some sort of fit, presumably similar to those experienced by my girls. In Meissen, Germany, around the beginning of the 1900s, a girl's hands began trembling whilst writing. Over a period of about six months, over two hundred children were afflicted with the same disorder. In Louisiana, America, near the beginning of the second world war, a schoolgirl developed pain and twitching in her leg; the condition spread until many other girls in the school developed the same thing. There are many other examples. It's all just bizarre. Extraordinary." He paused.

"Do go on," said Julian.

"Well, I don't know how much you know about these things but I can tell you that, the more one reads, the more one becomes enthralled and, frankly, worried. One episode that occurred in Malaysia about the 1970s particularly struck me. Many students at a school reported that they had seen a black figure lurking in the shadows. They stated that they felt something supernatural was trying to enter their bodies; it was causing physical symptoms and disturbing their minds."

"So what do you conclude from all this?" said Julian, dispassionately but with mounting inner interest.

"Well, of course I don't know," said the headmaster, "and I am not the sort of person to engage in flights of fancy. But is it possible - just possible - that there is some other explanation for all these bizarre things that have been going on, obviously for a long period of time ? Another explanation, apart from that offered by the doctors, I mean."

"Any ideas?"

"I hesitate to suggest anything, Mr. Harcourt-Brown, because I like to think I am a rational man. Please treat anything I say as the sort of imaginative ramblings that might go on between two men in a pub after a couple of pints!" He laughed.

"I am used to that sort of conversation," said Julian, "so I might just be in my element!"

"Well, the incidents that happened in New Amboise, Illinois in 1948, that I referred to earlier are particularly interesting. I looked at these in as much depth as I was able from the information I could find because they were mentioned specifically by Dr. Soames as having particular parallels with the goings-on at our school."

John Cartwright went on to describe the history of the Mystery Gasser and how girls in particular were affected; the possibility of the girls being affected by accidental poisoning but how no toxin could be identified; and the evidence that they may have been in some form of chronic stress state.

"But this is what struck me as particularly interesting," said the headmaster, "although I would not wish to put too much interpretation upon it: the locals put the blame upon a woman in the town, who they said was carrying out acts of evil. That, in itself, may not be too surprising because there have been witch hunts throughout history but what is remarkable is that the episodes of supposed gassing ceased abruptly when the woman was ousted from the town. Coincidence? Or not?"

By the time Julian left the headmaster, he felt he had fulfilled a useful function. John Cartwright had bottled up his anxieties about the school and the girls in it and his mind had been whirring with wonder for some time with no place for release. Julian, as a complete stranger, who would probably never be seen again in the village, acted as the perfect sounding board, especially when he managed to convince the headmaster of total discretion. Hopefully now Mr. Cartwright would have achieved some sense of balance and ability to approach the problems of his school with calm rationality. True, Julian had not offered much in the way of opinion but he knew that a good listener is sometimes all it is necessary to be.

And what had Julian gained from it all? Probably more than John Cartwright would think; at least, thoughts of strange women - and more thoughts of Charlotte.

As he left the school, he realised that he was surprisingly affected by the story of the mass fainting attacks related by the headmaster.   In an uncommonly low mood, he wandered aimlessly around the village streets for maybe twenty or thirty minutes.   He gained some comfort when he found himself, without conscious intent, standing on the bridge over the river, hands on the parapet, looking at the water flowing away beneath him.   There had been heavy rain on the hills over the preceding few weeks and the river was in full swell.   The tumbling of the water over the rocks of the river bed and the thick foliage that bordered its banks created a soothing pattern and yet the memory of the girls' trauma - so many of them - heightened his sense of vulnerability and the seeming random way in which misfortune strikes.   It was not long before the calming sense provided by the running water gave way to an associated fear of danger.   *How easy it would be for someone to slip on the river bank and fall into that torrent.   Unless they had a very powerful physique, they would surely drown.*

But then he reminded himself that he had spent his whole professional life listening to and reporting on disaster.   He straightened himself up from the parapet, took a deep breath and walked on.   *This was nothing new.   And yet...   And yet, in so many ways it was.   OK, be positive: as usual, I will research it.   The headmaster had given me some impetus.   What he told me was that similar things had happened before in other places.   Maybe there was more of an answer than the headmaster had discovered.   It's got nothing to do with the missing girl - at least, I think - but at least it gives me a bit of a break.*

His scanning the shelves of the non-fiction section in the local village library and combing the pages of all the available encyclopaedias there yielded nothing.   But something led him not to let it rest. He vowed to search the newspaper archives on his return to London.

Julian sat down at his office desk and turned on his computer. He prided himself on working for a newspaper group that was at the forefront in the use of technology in journalism. Yes, the traditional methods of researching a good story remained the most important because nothing could replace the word of mouth from a witness, particularly when delivered in a language or tone that would excite the reader when written out for them and placed into context using skills that only a journalist has. But, in order to provide a background, knowledge of events that had led up to the main reported story and any relevant, similar events from the past required access to historical newspaper articles. It was here that his employers had had the vision to start a project whereby all previous editions of their newspapers and their contents would be catalogued and indexed in a computer database. The project was not complete and often it was necessary to go back to hard copies or microfiches but there was no doubt it had already transformed the way that he and his fellow journalists worked.

Mass hysteria was the term that the doctor had used. Ok, let's see what we get.

He typed "mass hysteria" into the search box and few results showed up but one, relating to three articles from 1980, seemed of particular importance. He jotted down the references and walked down to the basement where the main archives were housed. He drew up the microfiches. *Here it is.*

"Tuesday 26 August 1980. The latest information on the mystery illness that affected children at the Hollinwell show this year and reported by this newspaper on 14th July suggests that the cause was some sort of psychological reaction that spread amongst the band members. The official report of the incident has concluded that the episodes of fainting that ultimately affected maybe 300 people were an example of so-called mass hysteria."

"Our correspondent has had the opportunity to interview one of the authors of the report, a medical doctor, who states that mass hysteria often develops as a sudden panic reaction, for whatever reason, in one individual and the panic then causes physical symptoms, such as fainting. The panic spreads to those around her (the cases are usually female) who go on to develop the same physical symptoms. So the cause of the physical symptoms is entirely due to something going on in the mind." Pretty much what the doctor told the headmaster.

"Amazing though it sounds, this is apparently not the first example of its kind. We summarise below some of the remarkable events from the past, in which numerous people have been afflicted by a mystery illness the cause of which is now believed to be mass hysteria."

Julian paused and, before reading on, extracted the July article from the archive.

"Monday, 14 July 1980. The Hollinwell Show, an annual event at the showground near Kirkby-in-Ashfield, took place on Sunday 13 July. The Forest League of Juvenile Jazz Bands was in attendance and organised a junior brass and marching competition. About five hundred children from eleven marching bands across the East Midlands entered the competition, sometimes coming from as far as forty miles away."

"All seemed to be going well but, around the middle the morning, some of the band members began to faint for no obvious reason. The illness seemed to spread rapidly so that at one point, according to an eye witness, the children were collapsing "like nine pins". Eventually, nearly 300 victims were identified. Most have been taken to nearby hospitals, including the Queen's Medical Centre, Nottingham, and some have been detained overnight. The cause of the illness, affecting so many young people, remains so far unexplained but the local authority assures us that a full enquiry will be made."

Julian returned to the later article from August 1980 and read on.

"We summarise below just some of the remarkable events from the past, in which numerous people have been afflicted by a mystery illness, the cause of which has never, until recently, been satisfactorily explained."

"Writing tremor epidemic, Gross-tinz and Basel, Switzerland (1892, 1904)

In 1892, in Gross-tinz, a ten-year-old girl developed shaking of one hand whilst writing and went on to have seizures affecting the whole body. Nineteen other students were affected. in Basel, another twenty were similarly afflicted in the same year and nearly thirty further children in a separate outbreak twelve years later. "

"Bellevue, Louisiana (1939)

A seventeen-year-old girl developed twitching of one leg at a dance. The condition soon spread to many other girls, who experienced jerking movements on their legs, chest and neck."

"Tanganyika laughing epidemic (1962)

At a boarding school in Tanzania, three girls began laughing seemingly involuntarily. The symptoms spread through the school until nearly one hundred teenagers were similarly affected. The involuntary laughter persisted in some cases for up to sixteen days. Eventually the school was closed. The laughing symptoms then recurred in a village that was home to some of the girls and later to two other schools."

"Welsh, Louisiana (1962)

Twenty-one teenage girls and one boy at a school were affected by seizures over a period of six months."

"Over the years, many theories have been put forward to explain these strange events, including viral infections, poisoning and even the actions of witches but experts have never been able to find enough evidence to pinpoint any particular cause. This latest report from Hollinwell suggests that many, if not all, are examples of mass hysteria. We will continue to report any new developments in this fascinating and disturbing saga."

Actions of witches? Really? Can anybody truly think that? Isn't this the twentieth century, after all? Anyway, it looks as if we now have some sort of scientific explanation. Interesting reading but nothing much more to add to what the headmaster has found. I guess the poor girls at the Combe Hollow School have nothing to do with the missing girl, anyway. And yet...and yet... what was it that caused Charlotte to leave so suddenly? Come on, Julian - anything but witches! Just keep looking, with an open mind, and find the answer.   You can do it - remember, you've done it before.

Julian had returned to Hackney to pursue the second strand of his story. First thing was to speak to the police.

Yes, explained the police sergeant, after examining the records, he did remember the case of the missing girl and the tragedy of her boyfriend that followed it. But there was never any suggestion of criminal intent on her part or of anyone else. She was recorded as a missing person - and indeed still is - but the investigations that can be carried out in such cases, where no criminal act is involved, are limited. They had done as much as they could but could find no substantial evidence from witness statements or search of her flat to indicate where or why she had left. No further police activity was planned unless further evidence came to light and so the case remained dormant on file.

After producing the articles he had written for the press about the time of her disappearance and confirming his identity, Julian had little difficulty in persuading the policeman to allow him access to the limited information available, especially if it led to resolution of the case. The police are always keen to close cases, he knew, if only, to be realistic, because it improved their record and they did not have the resources available to put further effort into this one. Julian opened the box file and quickly thumbed through the pieces of paper that the police had collected from the flat before reaching deeper into the file and withdrawing a photograph.

"Is this her?" he asked.

"We believe so," said the officer, "because the man who has his arm around her in the picture is certainly the man who died on the railway track; it is the same person who is in another photograph that was on display in the flat - that one is further down in the file - and the picture matches the description of the missing girl provided by her neighbours. I think we can say confidently that that is her."

"May I take these papers?"

"I am sorry, sir, but we cannot allow them to leave the police premises, at least as long as the case remains on file. But you are welcome to examine them in more detail here in the station for as long as you need. You can take a seat in the interview room, where there is a table, if you wish."

"Thank you. I will do that. But the photograph - may I at least take the photograph because that would obviously be very helpful in my search for her outside this area where people may well not know her."

"I probably shouldn't, strictly speaking," said the sergeant, "but we did make copies of the original photograph for several officers to use during our initial search and I could let you have one of those. I can understand that it would be very helpful."

Julian slipped the photograph into his briefcase and took a seat at the table provided. After an hour or so of diligently examining electricity bills and random grocery receipts, he lifted the next item from the box, another electricity bill, folded in two. As he opened it, a small piece of white notepaper fell onto the table. Nothing of note except a few scribbles in pencil: *Thurs D 8 32 A 11 18*. He copied the few details onto his own notepad and pondered.

Julian was used to trying to draw conclusions from fragments of evidence because a good newspaper story did not depend so much on establishment of hard facts but more on what seemed a plausible conclusion from the evidence available. In this respect, perhaps, he felt that he sometimes had the edge on the police who pursue their investigations in an orderly manner, moving from one piece of hard evidence to another. After all, a criminal case has to be founded on material that is beyond reasonable doubt whereas a newspaper story simply has to sound credible.

Thurs is clearly Thursday, he thought. *And 8 32 and 11 18 are probably times.* It took him just a couple of minutes to work out the rest. *The whole thing is pretty damned obvious, isn't it? They are departure and arrival times. Why didn't the police work that one out? Maybe they did not see the paper wrapped up in an old bill and maybe they stopped looking diligently, as I almost did, when they became bored to tears looking at electricity and grocery bills.*

Julian acknowledged to himself that he did not know for sure to which period of time the presumed journey related but it was one of nearly three hours and must therefore have been something special. A few enquiries amongst her neighbours would establish fairly quickly whether she had been on any such journey before she left for good. If not, then there was a good chance that the times on the paper refer to her final exit from the neighbourhood.

He headed back to the mini-supermarket, half hoping that the woman whom he had doubted so much at their first encounter might be there again. It might be, just be, that she was a fount of information, even if most of it was intuitive.

Intuition was, after all, what he relied on so much in his profession that he could hardly doubt that others may share the skill. Assuming it was sound. Sadly, he had also met a lot of people in his job who were willing to share their opinions founded on not much more than pure air; the conspiracy theorists were the worst. But at least she was someone who obviously kept her eyes open and realistically might well know whether Jennie had taken a journey somewhere.

She was not there. But maybe he should have realised that the proprietor of the shop, despite his avowed scepticism and rebuttal of gossip, nevertheless took in what his clients fed to him in addition to his own observations.

"Hello again," he said.

"You remember me?" said Julian.

"Yes, of course; I remember most people who come into my shop."

Julian picked up a chocolate bar and a bottle of fizzy drink from the counter and, with the payment, handed them to the man, hoping that the gesture might, in its small way, open up the proprietor's heart.

"You remember my asking about the missing girl?"

"Very much."

"I don't have much more to ask you," said Julian with deliberate softness of voice, "but would you mind telling me if you have any knowledge of her having taken a long journey somewhere, a journey of perhaps three hours there and three hours back at any time before she disappeared?"

"I am sure she did not. It's not only that I never heard her mention anything like that but she also came in here fairly often and I don't remember her being away for any length of time.

Also, I have my reliable collection of confidantes - or gossip-mongers, some might call them - who come regularly to the shop and tell me what is going on around here. I think one or other of them would have told me if there was something so devastatingly important!" He burst into laughter. Julian's suspicions were confirmed and it seemed likely that the man's opinion was correct.

It could be a coach or even a boat but wouldn't someone choosing to escape at short notice most likely choose the train? And to escape as far as they reasonably could - and at a cost they could afford - would the train not be the obvious choice? And a journey of about three hours? Yes, the train was the most likely.

And so, in the comfort of his hotel room, Julian scanned the railway timetables. Leaving from London - *that's pretty obvious.* But how many trains, from all the London stations, left at 8:32 and arrived somewhere - yes, where, that's the critical point - at 11:18 on a Thursday? There must be hundreds - and then what would he do?

But there were not. There was one.

Can it be true? Just one? Julian checked and checked again but got the same result: just one. He stood up and stretched backwards with his hands clasped behind his head, then paced around the room, intermittently extending his head and laughing. Then he stopped and laughed even more. *Eureka - just one!*

The 8:32 left King's Cross Station every Thursday and, at 11:18, arrived in York. *York, here we come!*

Chapter 7

York, England 1999

Jennie could not change her whole person but she could change her appearance and her identity. Now Helen Collins, over three months her hair had changed to dark brown; her face was bedecked with non-functional spectacles; she had gained fourteen pounds in weight and her clothes had become decidedly more drab, mostly ankle-length dresses in browns and olive green, accompanied by a simple cardigan of equally neutral colour.

Her residence in York was selected for its position away from the main streets but sufficiently close to people on whom she could call in an emergency. But only in an emergency for, the rest of the time, she chose deliberately to be as far away from the public eye as possible. Yes, she had to work to live but she had been fortunate to get a job with a mail order firm that allowed her to carry out most of the business from the security of her own home. The nearby corner shop was able to provide virtually all of her daily needs and she trusted the quiet, middle-aged, stocky proprietor as a model of confidentiality; this man certainly did not seem keen on talking to his customers more than necessary, in particular refusing to answer when one of them began to engage in idle gossip. Her life appeared under control - at least, as much as it could be.

She knew she was lonely and cutting herself completely from her previous life was not easy. How she wished that the brain did not have capacity for memories that intruded into her consciousness, uncalled for, at regular intervals throughout each and every day. Her life in the village, her friends and, more recently, James - James! How could she have done that to him, to have wrapped him up in her life, a life that she knew at the time was one of escape, of danger? Well, she told herself, she had no choice because love does not respect logic or common sense and it struck her and him when she did not ask it to. But was it love to leave him without explanation, to abandon him to his despair? At the time, it seemed as if it was; it was made clear to her that, if she did not get out of his life, he would suffer from some perverted influence that was out to destroy her and everything that was close to her. And how could she foresee the later terrible consequences to him that she read about in the newspapers? At least, she hoped that he suffered less in that way than he would have done had she stayed. And her father, her darling Daddy, to whom she had recently drawn much closer she had abandoned just when he needed her most.

Although troubled by these recurrent, intruding emotions, Helen's conscious mind was resigned to a perpetual, simple life from now on. Her small flat was comfortable; the man, Paul, in her friendly corner shop had agreed to buy in books on demand just for her whenever she needed one so she read avidly; and her need for human contact, which fortunately was not great, was satisfied by her studying from her window the passers-by in the street below. Occasionally, she would venture to a service at the nearby Minster, a place where she felt surely God would keep her safe.

Usually, Helen would ask Paul for books that she had seen recommended in magazines or newspapers but sometimes he would take it upon himself to bring ones that he thought she would like. Usually, he was not far off the mark because he had learned enough about her tastes from her own requests and, even when not quite to her liking, she would read the book with enthusiasm for she saw his actions as a gesture of friendliness in an otherwise barren life. That background in itself seemed to add warmth and interest to the novels that he brought. But when he handed her "The Witch of Blackbird Pond" by Elizabeth George Speare, she had to admit some surprise.

"A book about witches, Paul? It doesn't sound quite like the happy-ever-after ones I usually read." She thought back to the witch exhibition she went to with James at the British Museum. "I'm honestly not sure I should read it." But he was persistent.

"Well, someone told me it was very good and she's not the miserable type. Apparently, it won a prize! I thought you might like to try something a bit different. Anyway, technically it's a children's book so it can't be all that miserable. I gather lots of adults read it too so I thought you might give it a try. I'll take it back if you'd rather."

Faithful to perhaps her only friend in her new world, Helen took the book but had no intention of reading it. The experience in the museum was enough and, whilst she did not believe in witches, she had no wish to do anything that might rekindle her feelings of persecution. She hoped, and was beginning to believe, that she had finally escaped and that her mind was now able to occupy itself with more normal things.

But she knew that Paul would ask her about the book about two weeks or so after he had given it to her, as he usually did. She could not lie blatantly to someone who had been so good to her so, one day, when she was sitting quietly by her window, she picked up the book with the intention of skimming through it and finding something tangible that she might be able to relate back to him, without having to read it all.

She read about Wethersfield, a town that becomes afflicted by a deadly illness and how a woman, Hannah, is accused of being a witch and causing the catastrophe. Helen was already tired when she skimmed through to that point in the story; she put down the book, rested her head back and closed her eyes. *How petty people can be, always blaming someone else when things go wrong in life. But it is only a story. And yet there is truth in it; that is what people are like. Always trying to find scapegoats, like I suppose calling people witches.*

Helen fell asleep for a few minutes but, when she awoke, related thoughts were drifting randomly through her mind. *Do witches really exist? Aren't they just girls and women who dress up in silly costumes at Halloween and form the subject of children's stories? Maybe to frighten the pants off them. No, children are smarter than that; they just laugh. But do they really exist? Maybe I don't know enough about witches.*

Helen cast her mind back to her home village, a place where she had grown up as a happy child, laughing with other children, dressing in witches' costumes and carrying turnip lanterns at Halloween. *My mother must have spent her hard-earned money on those silly costumes. What a waste. But then we were happy and that made her happy too. A lovely village, how distraught she was to have had to flee from it. Everything used to be so peaceful. Well, until those girls started passing out but the doctors seemed to think that was all in their mind. A reaction to stress or something like that. Why on earth would they all feel so stressed living there? Hormones maybe.*

But then there was also Megan, someone who had seemed so friendly to her and her parents and especially after her mother disappeared. How can people change so much? And so insidiously? How can anyone change to become controlling, threatening and frightening to the extent that she had had to leave the village to get away from her? Was it Megan that was responsible for the terror unleashed upon her in Hackney, that caused her to abandon her love in the belief that it was for his own sake, with tragic consequences? How could that be? *Maybe, like those schoolgirls, I am just going mad.*

She started to feel sleepy again. As she dozed off for a second time, one thought recurred: *Or maybe a witch after all.*

After Julian had dismounted from the train and walked through the York station approach, he headed towards the city centre. Partly to research the area but more to focus his mind, he decided to take a walk around. He had been to York before but only once and that was a long time ago; some sort of conference, he remembered, when he was at the debut of his career. But now the time and purpose were different.

He crossed the River Ouse over Lendal Bridge, turned right and then left onto Stonegate. He gazed into the shop windows for a few minutes before heading into Davygate. Over to the right was Bettys Tea Rooms. A vision of his treating himself to afternoon tea there many years ago flashed across his mind; things seemed so much easier then. After turning left and then deliberately moving towards the smaller, more characterful streets, he found himself in The Shambles and stopped for a few minutes to study the mediaeval, timber-framed buildings that overlooked the street.　Hanging from one of the buildings nearby was an old butcher's hook.

This place is so full of history, so charming.　He imagined himself, dressed in sixteenth-century costume, tending to slabs of meat at the side of the road and cutting into joints in full view of the passing public.　No cars, no planes, no trains.　An idyllic, simple lifestyle, he thought.　But then: of course it was not; no real doctors, no antibiotics, no sewage facilities, people dying young.　And probably just as much crime, maybe more.　And people being imprisoned in dungeons and executed for trivial crimes, or maybe even no crimes at all, just at the fancy of someone in power who took exception to them or listened too hard to someone else who had taken a dislike to them.　*Like the witches.　The witches - why do they keep popping up?　But, while I think about it, they are the classic example - people who might have been a bit odd, different from the others, who were blamed for evil-doing whenever something went wrong. Hopefully, things have now moved on although the more I listen to people, the more I wonder.　Maybe we - or they, hopefully I'm different - just wrap the same feelings up in some more sophisticated guise but still take things out on other people for no reason.　Oh dear; let's move on.*

Now was the time to start his proper work.　Where would she have chosen to live?　Of course, it could have been somewhere out of town or even further away.　Maybe she had got another train from York, a taxi or some other transport and who knows where that would have taken her?　But first he had to hope that York was her final destination; if not, the whole search process would have to start anew.

He continued his walk around the city but, this time, the soaking in of culture, reflections on the past and simply trying to clear his mind had to take second place. Now he had to focus and focus in particular on the letting agencies dotted around town. She must have rented somewhere; she must have gone to a letting agency; she would not have had time or probably energy to search through private advertisements. And she likely would have chosen one that she found as she wandered from the station through the town. He wrote them all down in his notebook as he passed through the streets and then systematically went back to each one in turn. What did he have to go on? A young girl from London who arrived alone on a Thursday, who might have appeared a little distressed and with an urgent need for accommodation. Probably she had little luggage. And there was the photograph.

One after another, the same pattern: his repeating the same lines and the girl in the letting agency, for it was usually a girl, staring intently at the photograph and then looking him in the eyes, shaking her head and stating that she did not think she recognised the person. After five or six agencies, Julian reflected that he was so adept at giving his pattered speech with imploring tones and facial expression that maybe, somewhere in his life, he had overlooked a talent and missed a thriving career in the theatre. His requests for the girls to consult others in their office, who may have dealt with the missing girl, were also universally unproductive because apparently the other staff were out on visits or in meetings. No, sadly, he explained, he could not leave the photograph behind to show them later because it was his only copy. But he was grateful for their offer for him to come back later when the other staff may be available.

He was battling with a mounting feeling of dispiritedness but pressed on. He walked over Ouse Bridge onto Micklegate and wandered casually and slowly down the street, examining the several estate agents to find the one that seemed most likely to be helpful but, of course, it was impossible to know. Feeling the need for some relief of effort, he was gratefully distracted by, in the distance, the imposing edifice of Micklegate Bar, an ancient gate into the town; he walked over to look. It was hard not to be impressed: twin, tall, circular turrets of stone, bedecked with coats of arms, flanked by the city walls and pierced by several arches. *Yet more grand history - and yet, no doubt, more barbarism. How many heads had been hung from those parapets as examples to others? And for any good reason? Quite possibly not. Maybe even some witches.* This latest quest, the search for a girl with no history, was, without doubt, stimulating his imagination more than most others. Perhaps it was necessary because not often had he had to deal with a case quite so mysterious and unexplained.

Julian walked back down Micklegate towards the estate agent he had chosen as first visit on that street. He stopped at the entrance and examined the property advertisements in the display windows to ensure that they let as well as sold properties and then walked in. Just one person sitting at a desk, as always, who no doubt was on holiday or otherwise indisposed on the day that our missing girl arrived or, for whatever reason, had no memory of such a person and no-one else was available. He prepared himself for the usual conversation and the usual outcome but knew he had to continue.

Maybe it was because this lady receptionist was older and perhaps therefore more interested in the plight of young girls on their own, seeking accommodation; maybe at the time she perceived her distressed state even if it was disguised; but, for whatever reason, there was no doubt that, more than most, she was interested and prepared to put her mind to Julian's enquiry.

"As a matter of fact, I think I do recognise that girl," she said peering closely at the photograph and frowning. "But I don't remember him."

"No, sorry, this is the only photograph I have of her. He definitely would not have been with her."

"Of course, sorry, I am being stupid. You have already said she was alone."

"Which makes me think. We do not get many young girls looking for rental property on their own. Usually they are with a boyfriend or one of a group of girls who want to house-share or flat-share. So that might be why she stands out in my memory." She paused.

"Not only that, now I think. There was a girl I seem to remember who was a bit agitated. She'd just arrived in York and needed a place urgently. As long as it was quiet, she didn't much care where it was as long as she could walk everywhere she needed. In fact, she was happy to take somewhere without even going to look at the choice we had on offer. And that's unusual. I cannot be sure it was the same girl; I might be mixing up the two. Though, as I said, we don't get that many girls on their own looking for places."

"Is there any way you can trace her through your records?"

"I think you have already said that you don't have her name."

"Sadly not. Her first name could have been Jennie or Charlotte but, from what I know, she may well have changed her name a few times. Her original surname was Black but she very likely changed that too."

"Do you know her date of birth?"

"No, I do not. Wait, but hang on a minute! I am pretty sure she was twenty-two - possibly twenty-one - when she left her original home - which was in Combe Hollow in the Cotswolds, by the way. She left about this time last year so she must have been born in 1976 or 1977. Does that help?"

"And when do you think she came here?"

"Don't know - much more than I said - several months ago." *How stupid - if I had thought, I could probably have found out exactly when she left Hackney. Obviously it was shortly before the boyfriend died on the railway line. And you wrote about this, for goodness sake.* "Actually," he continued, "it was probably around March. I could probably find out more precisely, if it would be helpful." *Why did you not bring your original article with you?*

"OK but first let me look through our records from, say, the last year to see if we let to a single girl with that year of birth. It may take me a little while. Could you come back tomorrow?"

With renewed and unexpected optimism, Julian smiled affectionately towards his new-found informant and left, promising to return as planned. The afternoon was moving into the evening. Now was the time to relax and reflect. First, a quick walk around the town to clear his head again; then a call at an off licence he passed earlier, followed by return with a bottle to his hotel room and a relaxing dinner in the restaurant. Not a special menu but adequate under the circumstances, especially if primed with a little wine.

Jennie returned to her flat from the corner shop, carrying a plastic bag of groceries, as usual enough to last her the week so that she did not have to venture out too often. It was approaching six o'clock and the familiar dull gloom of many autumn afternoons was closing in so that, by now, her apartment, with its small windows, would likely be in semi-darkness, She turned the key in the lock of her front door and instinctively reached to the side to turn on the hall light. But, when she saw the light streaming under the adjacent sitting room door, she froze. *No, I didn't leave it on when I left; I never do. I make sure I never do. Or could I possibly have done just this once?* And had she put the light on when she returned home from work and before she left straight away for the shop? *Did I? I can't remember.*

Well, she rationalised, nobody could have got in. Her landlord always called her before visiting and he was the only one, apart from her, with a key. Anyone breaking in would have to climb up the outside of the building to the third floor and would surely raise suspicion amongst passers-by. Even though the street was relatively quiet, there was certainly a regular stream of people going about their business outside her apartment window, particularly at this time of day, when many would be on their last bit of journey from work to home. *No, I must have left the light on.*

With greater confidence, she walked purposefully towards her sitting groom and opened the door.

"Hello Jennie."

Jennie did not need to react because she had prepared at least in some measure for this moment, abhorrent though it was to her every thought, and one that she had taken every step possible to avoid; that much she knew. She managed to remain calm, at least for a while.

"Why are you here? What do you want?"

"They took my daughter and now I want her back."

"I don't have your daughter. What do you want from me?"

"I want you. I have been searching, searching, and now I have found you. You are my daughter and I want you back."

Although she had heard it before, the suggestion, absurd though it was, that she could somehow be related at all to this creature, let only be her daughter, still impacted on her mind. Jennie could no longer hold her restraint, although sense told her to try to be rational. She screamed, her voice trembling: "You are wrong, it's not me you want, I am not you daughter, please understand. You are mistaken. Really, I am not your daughter."

"You are now. And you will come with me."

The woman was standing in the centre of Helen's sitting room. The mystery of how she had got there when Helen obsessively ensured that her doors and windows were always locked and there was no sign of a break-in no longer seemed important. An ordinary looking, unassuming figure, dressed in a grey, calf-length skirt and darker grey bolero jacket; a face of little expression yet nonetheless determined; but a voice that belied her appearance in its quiet but cutting stridency. The eyes held fixed gaze through the round glasses. A somewhat different appearance but nevertheless the same person, the woman she feared.

"Do you want to know why I am here?" she said.

"Of course I do! I have told you: there is nothing you could want from me. I have done nothing to harm you and, yes, you are frightening me. Why do you persist in persecuting me? I beg you - please, please leave me alone."

"You are coming with me, I can assure you, because the alternative you will not be able to bear. But first, yes, I will tell you why I am here." Jennie sat down.

"They killed my daughter, my poor innocent daughter, who had done no harm to them or anyone else in this world or beyond. She was a sickly child but they could not see it and they pursued her, pursued her to her death. And why? Because they decided that she had done a pact with the Devil. Well, one thing has been certain since then and that is that I will not rest until I have seen her death avenged. That has been my purpose in this world since they took her away from me. And I will see it through. If my child must suffer for her innocence, then so will the daughters of others so that the world can see what, in its misguidedness, it has inflicted upon itself. And not only that but I will get my daughter back and she can join me in my mission."

"But I am not your daughter!"

"You are the replacement for her. If I cannot have that which has been taken away from me, I will have the next best thing. And that is you. And with you I will have her spirit."

"Why can you not just find your daughter's spirit?"

"I have. It is in you."

Jennie breathed deeply several times and resumed her calm. She looked up from her chair into the eyes of her pursuer. "When and where did all this happen?"

"When and where did this happen? Do you really want to know? Well, if you want to know, I will tell you. It was on a mission to Lourdes in June 1880. My daughter was seeking healing from the Virgin Mary. But that was not to be. They destroyed her and God did not come to her rescue."

"You could not have been alive in 1880 - no-one lives that long!" Helen was now coming to the realisation more than ever that her tormentor might be seriously deranged - and therefore unpredictable - and she began to panic again.

"With my Master, all things are possible. His missionaries do not live life as you know it - but you would not understand. Space and time mean nothing to us. However, when you come with me, then you will be one of us and all will be clear."

"And supposing I don't?"

"You have seen the revenge that has been wreaked on the girls in your own neighbourhood. And there are others in different parts of the world that you do not know about. All this has been necessary and a consequence of the destruction that they imparted upon my child, while I searched for her. And, no, I am not sorry for what I have done. Now I have found her and, when she - you - come with me, there will be no need for it to carry on. But if you do not, I tell you that the revenge will be so much worse. You will see harm to girls throughout the world that you could never even dream of."

"I tell you I am not your daughter!"

"Listen!" She glared. "Do you know that, in America, in a place called New Amboise maybe fifty years ago, a town was plagued by what they liked to call the Mad Gasser?" She laughed. "Many, many girls suffered attacks in the night when they could not breathe and became paralysed. They never found out what caused it and, of course, they would not. They drove me out of the town and no doubt felt proud of it because all their troubles stopped then. But that does not mean anything to me. I just appear somewhere else in the world and no-one can ever stop me doing that because I have the power of the Master. And listen to this: do you know that, fifteen years ago, hundreds of girls in Palestine started fainting for no obvious reason? They thought they had been poisoned but could not prove it. Not surprising, really." She laughed again. "And then the poor girls who could not stop their teeth chattering, the ones who could not stop laughing, the mysterious cuts and rashes, the uncontrollable dancing. Heartbreaking, isn't it?"

"And again let me remind you, Jennie, there's your sweet, little village of Combe Hollow. Such a shame about those girls."

"Did you cause all that?"

"I just showed those girls that life is fragile and that they and their parents need to get out of their smug, self-satisfied comfort zones. But they are lucky. At least I let the girls stay alive, which is more than I can say for what they did to my daughter. I might not be able to replace her in body but you are the next best thing. And you will come with me."

"How can you say that? That I am the next best thing? You do not know me; you know nothing about me, even if it possible that I might look a bit like your daughter. Looking like your daughter does not make me a replacement for her. There must be thousands of people who look a bit like her. What about me, the real me? You know nothing about that."

"The body is not important. I know your spirit and that is what makes you her. And that is what I want. Your spirit is the spirit of my daughter."

"Those girls never did you any harm. Why did you want to hurt them?"

The woman's eyes opened wide and seemed almost to blaze with fury; she spat out her words with vitriol.

"Revenge, Jennie, revenge! Revenge is sweet - you have heard that said and now I can tell you just how sweet it really is. It is very sweet, very sweet indeed! If they can do the vilest of things to my daughter, who was innocent, then I can do the same to the innocent daughters of others. My daughter never did anybody any harm but they wanted to hurt her. No, more than that - they wanted to destroy her - and they did. So they can take the consequences of their vile actions by seeing that other innocent girls can also come to harm when they have done nothing to deserve it. But I told you - none of those girls has died - not yet. What I have done to them is a kindness in comparison to what they did to my daughter."

"And I will also tell you this: I have been everywhere, Jennie, all around the world, looking for you. I admit to having been frustrated and I tell you I do not like to be frustrated. The greater the frustration, the more the need for revenge."

Jennie's body suddenly stiffened in a horrifying realisation. "Did you kill my mother?"

"She was in the way, Jennie. She was so protective of you, she stopped me getting close to what was mine. Always in the way, Jennie, always in the way. She believed that you belonged to her and that I could not be tolerate."

210

Jennie started to tremble and cry but then she forcefully regained her composure and looked up into the face of her pursuer.

"Are you a witch?"

"If that is what you want to call it. That is what they called my daughter. They accused her of collaborating with the Evil One. For no reason. Well, if they were looking for one who sides with the Devil, then I made it my mission to provide them with one. Everything that has happened to those girls is a consequence of the evil that they imparted to my poor innocent child. An eye for an eye and a tooth for a tooth - remember? Well, there it is. But now is your chance to put a stop to it all. Come with me. But, as I have said, if you do not, then all hell will break out - perhaps more literally than you think."

"Where do you want to take me?"

"When you come with me, I will have no more need to appear on this earth. You and I will be together in the world of spirits."

"If you believe you have fulfilled your mission, why don't you just stay here and go back to normal?"

"There is no going back when you have devoted yourself to the Master. I will have other work to do. I cannot come back, which is why you have to come with me."

"So am I going to die?"

"Life and death have no meaning in the spirit world. We can come and go as we please. We can appear at once anywhere on the earth and disappear just as quickly. But I cannot remain permanently on this earth, which is why you must come with me."

Jennie began to cry again but the witch took her hand and led her away.

Chapter 8

Julian's hotel room was not grand but comfortable. At least, he thought, he could walk from the door and sit in a chair without having to struggle around the end of the bed, like so many hotels he had stayed in, and the table was conveniently situated to accommodate his wine glass by his right hand when he sat down. Yes, he thought, on reflection he could be optimistic. He had found a helpful person and, with luck, she would dig out the details of the girl she remembered and, with a bit more luck, it will be Charlotte - *Jennie* - and then he would have her address; she will be found and the mystery of what she had been through will be uncovered. Perhaps he may even be able to help her. And meanwhile, he had some wine. *What more could I want right now?*

The first glass of sauvignon blanc went down rather quickly, he had to admit, but he excused himself that he had used those few minutes usefully, in glancing through the restaurant menu that was propped up on the table next to his glass. *Well, not necessarily the restaurant; the room service menu looks much the same. I'll decide later.* He poured a second glass. The third glass persuaded him to take the room service and, within thirty minutes, he was settling into the chilli con carne, an option he decided was least likely to be cooked badly. And then an early night.

As he expected, he fell asleep almost immediately on getting into bed. The first three hours passed without incident but, around one o'clock, a rushing feeling through his head woke him suddenly from sleep. He sat up abruptly, opened his eyes and started to reach for the bedside light but could see nothing, just complete blackness. He had deliberately left open the bedroom window and the curtains slightly apart to let fresh air into the room but the city lights that glimmered through the crack in the curtains were now replaced by total darkness. The illuminated digits on the bedside clock appeared extinguished.

But then, by the door, was a flash of light that settled immediately into a prolonged dull red glow. Julian stared at the swirling pattern upon the light's surface for what seemed like several minutes, trying to discern some recognisable shape and work out what logical explanation he could find for what he was experiencing. He tried to look around the rest of the room for some sort of answer but the red pattern held his gaze against all his efforts to shift it. He realised nevertheless that surprisingly he was not afraid.

After a few minutes more, an amorphous yellow patch developed in the middle of the red cloud and gradually developed form. Soon Julian was able to recognise facial features, eyes and a nose, and shortly afterwards the clear image of a complete face. And he knew who it was.

"Thank you for trying to help me, Julian, but it is too late," said Jennie. "She has taken me and I agreed to go. Now all will be well. You can now go home and live life normally."

"Who has taken you?" shouted Julian, with all rationale not expecting an answer.

"She who has been searching for me for many, many years. She who has caused such harm across the world in her efforts to find me. The witch. But now it will all stop."

"The witch! What witch?"

"It no longer matters, Julian. Just trust me. I have agreed to go with the witch so as to stop the persecution of other girls, persecution that has been going on for years, for decades."

"Tell me - who is this witch?"

"A witch, like any other. But now it is all resolved. Go home, Julian. Goodbye."

The face rapidly dissolved into an unrecognisable yellow patch against the red cloud and coalesced with it before the whole image faded and disappeared. Julian continued to stare but it had gone. He looked around the room; the city lights were twinkling through the gap in the curtains and the digital lights on the bedside clock read 1:47. Somehow, he returned to sleep.

At around six o'clock, he awoke as normal. The memory of the night was still firmly with him but he did not remember falling back to sleep or any dreams or other unusual happenings afterwards. He felt remarkably calm. *But I need to think and no doubt some caffeine would help.*

Back in bed with a cup of instant coffee on the table by the side of his empty wine glass, he purposefully positioned himself propped against two pillows, half sitting and half lying, and thought. Julian prided himself on his ability to think, free from distractions, mind cleared of irrelevancies and focussed on the issue he wanted to pursue. This was part of his professional life; his ability to do it had led to some of his best stories; and all he had to do now was use the same skills to come to terms with - no, resolve - what had happened just a few hours ago.

Obviously a dream and yet also obviously not. That's what they call a paradox. But more than that - a dream or not a dream, did it teach me something? Most likely my subconscious mind telling me to stop obsessing on the case of just one missing girl - when in truth there must be hundreds - and also telling me what I ought to know consciously, but refuse to accept, that I am not going to find the answer. As simple as that. He finished his coffee and, with firm determination, prepared for the day ahead and his plans to return to London.

But still in York, he decided he had not much more useful or interesting to do than finish what he had started there. He could go round the Castle Museum or take an early train home but he had promised the lady at the letting agency that he would go back and, if for no other reason than not to appear rude to someone who had been so helpful, he resolved to see through what he had started in this city. But when he reached another dead end, which no doubt he would, then he would go home and close down the affair in his mind.

"Yes," said the lady in the agency, "I have located her. Helen Collins. I dealt with her at the time and I made some notes, as I always do, but I also remember her well now. It's a bit odd that I haven't seen her since - well, not that I remember anyway - because most tenants call in soon after taking up their accommodation to sort out some minor detail or other. She did phone in a few times but mostly at our request. She always paid her rent in cash, usually dropping it through the letterbox when the office was closed."

"What do you remember about her?"

"Well, she looked pretty much like the photograph. As I think I said last time you were here, she seemed a bit agitated and keen to get things sorted out quickly. She couldn't provide any credit references but we agreed, a bit reluctantly I must admit, to accept a deposit in cash and let her move in on a monthly renewal. Fortunately, she found a job quickly and was able to prove her income so that was fine."

"Do you have an address?"

"Yes, it's a first floor flat on Goodramgate. Here are the details." She handed him one of the original property descriptions held on file. Julian offered her his profuse thanks and set off. He walked back across the Ouse, past Bettys - *maybe I can take afternoon tea there again when this is finished -* and down Stonegate towards the Minster. Although not naturally a very religious person, he studied the facade of the grand cathedral as he passed and could not help but reflect. Are they able to get rid of witches? *Obviously not, if they still exist.*

Next on Goodramgate, he was in close proximity to his destination, which was situated at the far end of the street. His expectations were to knock on the flat door, if he could get access to the building, or ring the outside bell or buzzer, if there was one; he would receive no answer and then he would make a few local enquiries to find that its occupant had fled suddenly for no obvious reason and, no, they did not know where she had gone. But the reality was different. Parked outside the flat building were two police cars; the door to the entrance was open and beside it stood a policeman, obviously guarding the entrance. As Julian got closer, an ambulance with its siren sounding came down the street from behind, passed him and stopped next to the police cars. Two paramedics got out and, with equipment in hand, were allowed by the police officer into the building with the instruction, "Flat 4, upstairs." *That's hers!*

Julian approached the policeman and showed him his identity card.

"Good morning, Officer. I am from the press - not the local press but the National Daily News. I am here in York researching the whereabouts of a missing person and I have reason to believe that she is living in this apartment building. I could not help overhear your instructions to the paramedics to go to Flat 4, which is the address I have been given for the person I am trying to find. May I ask you what is happening? May I go in?"

"I am sorry, sir, but this is currently designated a crime scene and I cannot allow you entry. A full statement will be given to the press when we have further information."

Julian's further attempts to extract even the most meagre of news from this source faced fierce resistance so he adopted a standard journalistic ploy, to interview the general public. He walked across the road to where a group of bystanders stood, waiting for the next development. But, on this occasion, the important tactic was not to divulge that he was from the press, a body on the whole distrusted by the man in the street. He adopted a casual approach.

"What's going on?"

"There's a girl lives there on her own," said a middle-aged man. "Something's happened to her. A woman in one of the other flats, I think the one underneath hers, heard shouting and screaming last night coming from the girl's flat. She thought it was just an argument between her and a boyfriend - although, to my knowledge, she doesn't have any - but, when this woman went out this morning, she noticed that the lights were still on and the curtains were open. And that's pretty unusual - the girl almost always has the lights off in the day and the curtains closed, well half-closed anyway."

"Do you live locally?"

"Yes, just over there," said the man, gesturing down the street.

"Do you know the girl?"

"No, not really, hardly ever saw her - nobody did. She kept herself to herself. But I know that it would be unusual for her to make a noise or to leave the lights on and curtains open and all that."

"Wow," said Julian with deliberate tone of surprise. "So the neighbour called the police?"

"Yes."

"But would you call the police just because someone left the lights on and so on?"

"Well, maybe not, but then there were those funny marks on the window - you can probably see them from here - and the lady thought they were marks of blood. I guess that's what persuaded her to call the cops."

Julian looked over to the first floor window: five large, cylindrical shapes extending up the window and an almost circular one beneath them, all in dusky red.

"It looks like a hand!" he said to his new-found companion.

"That's what I thought - and I imagine that's what the lady thought too and that's why she called the police. But if it is a hand, it's a pretty big hand, that's all I can say."

The two stared expectantly towards the flat until, about twenty minutes later, the paramedics reappeared, retrieved a stretcher from the ambulance and returned to the flat. A few minutes after that, they reappeared, the stretcher holding a body covered by a white sheet, and drove away with it in the ambulance. The policeman at the door and one other from one of the waiting cars entered the building and closed the door behind them.

"Well, that doesn't look too good," said the man on the pavement, "but I guess that's all we're going to find out for now. Seems like it's time to go. Nice meeting you - 'bye!" He turned on his heel and walked briskly away down Goodramgate.

No, that doesn't look good, thought Julian. *But he's probably also right that that's all we're going to find out for now.* As he watched the man walk down the street, Julian's mood sank abruptly. *Is this really the end of my journey? With still nothing properly explained?*

He felt powerless, frustrated and, with conscious surprise at his emotions, a deep caring for a girl he had never met and knew little about. In order to calm down, he began to walk.

He paced aimlessly up and down the street in front of the apartment building, intermittently gazing back up to the defiled window in horror and disbelief. But he knew that there was no rationale for his feelings, any more than in the saga he had explored with perhaps unreasonable diligence.

Sadly, Julian accepted what he had feared for some time. He had become absorbed with a story about a missing girl and her dead boyfriend for reasons that he could not easily explain; full of optimism, he had started out on a journey to find her and discover why she had disappeared. But, as time went on, he had become increasingly pessimistic that the full explanation would never be found. So why was he now so disappointed at an outcome that he had come latterly to predict? He did not know but one thing was now certain. If the girl being carried out of the flat was indeed the Charlotte he sought, and everything pointed to that conclusion, then he really had reached the end of the journey. The police might come up with the answer to what had led to her death but nothing he could do could advance the situation. This was indeed the end of his investigative journey. With a weary sigh, and slow in step, he slowly retraced his path down the street, returned to the hotel to check out and collect his belongings and headed off for the station. *What time's the train? Who cares, even if there isn't one for hours?*

Chapter 9

National Daily News, Thursday 17 October 1999
From our correspondent, Julian Harcourt-Brown

The whereabouts of a girl who went missing without trace from London and reported by this newspaper on 12 March this year may now have been solved although many questions remain. Charlotte, whose real name was Jennie Black, disappeared suddenly and inexplicably from Hackney, London that month and the body of her boyfriend was soon afterwards found on a local railway line. Without further evidence, the case went quiet until by fortune a letter, written by the girl, was discovered on a train travelling on the same line where the man died.

This newspaper took on further investigation and discovered that she had moved to Hackney from a sleepy Cotswold village, Combe Hollow, Gloucestershire and, not long afterwards, from London to York, where she lived alone in a small flat. It seems that her changes of residence were made suddenly and no-one is clear of the reasons for her sudden decisions to move.

On 3 October, the girl was found dead at her flat in York. She had no known enemies and, according to neighbours, lived a quiet solitary life in York. Criminal activity is not suspected and official postmortem reports have not identified a definite cause of death.

But it seems that the mystery does not end there. On the morning after the night that the girl died, eye witnesses noticed a large, red mark in the shape of a hand on the outside window of Jennie Black's flat. Forensic examination has confirmed that it is not blood but cannot identify of what the mark is composed. The body of the girl showed no signs of trauma except for several sets of three parallel lines, like scratches, on various parts of her body. The pathologists have no idea how they were made.

Our correspondent has had the opportunity to speak to experts in academic research of the occult who state that the marks on the window and the body of the girl are typical of many found over the centuries on bodies and buildings. Folklore has traditionally attributed these marks to visitations from the Devil but, of course, there has never been any proof. Readers can draw their own conclusions but sadly the fate of the missing girl now seems to be established and the remaining questions in this bizarre saga may never be answered.